S0-ACY-846

FAVORITE DOG STORIES

≫≫≫ WORLD JUNIOR LIBRARY ≪≪

Favorite Dog Stories

Edited by MARGUERITE BLOCH

Illustrated by ROBERT DOREMUS

CLEVELAND   NEW YORK

THE WORLD PUBLISHING COMPANY

Library of Congress Catalog Card Number: 50-6624

ACKNOWLEDGMENTS

The Publishers wish to acknowledge with thanks permission to use the following material contained in this volume:

"The 'Critter'" from *The Critter and Other Dogs* by Albert Payson Terhune. Copyright 1936 by Albert Payson Terhune. Reprinted by permission of Harper & Brothers.

"Kazan" from *Kazan* by James Oliver Curwood. Copyright 1914 by the Cosmopolitan Book Corporation. Copyright renewed 1941 by Ethel M. Curwood. Reprinted by permission of Rinehart & Company, Inc.

"That Spot" by Jack London. Copyright 1910 by Charmian London. Reprinted by permission of Mrs. London.

"Allegheny" from *Dumb-Bell and Others* by John Taintor Foote. Copyright 1919 by Crowell Collier Publishing Company. Copyright 1946 by John Taintor Foote. Reprinted by permission of Appleton-Century-Crofts, Inc.

"Lassie Come-Home" by Eric Knight. Copyright 1938 by The Curtis Publishing Company. Reprinted by permission of the Author's Estate. An expanded and novel-length form of this story is published at $2.50 by the John C. Winston Company.

"The Comet" from *Frank of Freedom Hill* by Samuel Arthur Derieux. Copyright 1922 by Doubleday & Company, Inc.

"Weep No More, My Lady" by James Street. Copyright 1945 by the author. Reprinted by permission of Harold Matson.

"Slipstream" from *A Man of His Own* by Corey Ford and Alastair MacBain. Copyright 1949 by the authors. Reprinted by permission of Whittlesey House.

HC 755

Copyright 1950 by The World Publishing Company. All rights reserved. No part of this book may be reproduced in any form without written permission from the publisher, except for brief passages included in a review appearing in a newspaper or magazine. Manufactured in the United States of America.

Contents

Preface

THE reader will encounter almost every sort of dog in the stories assembled here: domestic pets, sheep dogs, seeing eye and war dogs, heroes, hunters and huskies from the Arctic regions. And there are mutts and mongrels here, as well as the pure-bred aristocrats.

But more important than the breed and variety of the dogs in our "gallery" are the storytelling gifts and the affectionate understanding of dogs displayed by the authors who make up this book.

Dogs have been respected members of society since the Old Stone Age. We have records and pictures of them from ancient Greece, Assyria, Egypt and Rome. There are references to dogs in the Bible, the Talmud, ancient Chinese writings and in the literature of every land. Dogs have been bred for numerous uses and they have served man faithfully for many centuries. Primarily, though, the dog is the universal companion of man and child, and of all animals he is probably the most intelligent and affectionate.

Leigh Hunt once said of the dog: "One of the animals

which a generous and sociable man would soonest become is a dog. A dog can have a friend; he has affections and character, he can enjoy equally the field and the fireside; he dreams, he caresses, he propitiates; he offends, and is pardoned; he stands by you in adversity; he is a good fellow."

THE EDITOR

FAVORITE DOG STORIES

The "Critter"

"No," REFUSED Brand, "I'm not going to sell him and I'm not going to give him away, nor yet shoot him. I was planning to do one of the three, till I went to that Chautauqua lecture, down to Paterson. But ——"

"The only Chautauqua lecture, down there, that I was ever able to draw you to," interrupted his wife, "was the one on 'Small Beginnings of Great Men.' And ——"

"That's the one I'm talking about," said Brand.

"But what in the wide earth has that fine lecture got to do with this long-legged fool of a collie pup?" she demanded.

Amos Brand laughed sheepishly. Yet he stuck to his guns.

"Here's the idea," said he. "You remember how the lecturer chap said that Bismarck and Mr. Thackeray and Abraham Lincoln and two or three other great men were so lazy when they was young that nobody ever had any notion they'd be worth raising? He said young Abe Lincoln used to lie around and fish and read and swap funny stories and that he'd only hustle when he had to. He said Mr. Thackeray hadn't even got the energy to graduate from his college and that he spent his time there in gambling with cards. He said Bismarck was fonder of swigging lager beer in college than of learning his lessons and they packed him home as a dunce. He said ——"

"Oh, I remember all that!" put in his wife, impatiently. "But what has it got to do with ——?"

"He said," stolidly continued Amos—"he said all those fellers was some inches above six feet tall, and was built big in proportion, and they got their growth while they was youngsters; and the fast growing kept them from wanting to be of any use. Then when they had finished growing they cut loose and made big marks in the world."

"But ——"

"When we came home from the lecture, there was Leggy, standing at the gate, on the lookout for us. I stopped to take a good size-up of him. He's only six months old and he's a hand higher at the shoulder than old Shep, and he's got the legs of a yearling colt, and his strength is all laying around loose on him. As I set my eyes on him, here's the thought that comes to me:—'I'll bet that's how Mr. Thackeray (whoever he was) and Bismarck and grand old Abe Lincoln would have looked at his age, if they'd been collies. The poor cuss has grown so fast, he hasn't got the pep, left over, to amount to a hill of mildewed beans. If we keep him and treat him patient and kind, likely enough he'll shape into something that'll pay us back for the nine dollars we gave that professional breeder for him when he was five weeks old.' "

"Of all the crazy ——"

"Yes, Ruth, that's the very thought that come a-buzzing into my brain as I looked at him wagging his fool tail at me and looking like some ancestor of his had been a step-ladder or a clothes-pole. And it was a hunch. I'm going to play that hunch. Leggy is going to stay on here awhile, on the chance he'll turn out to be worth the powder and shot to blow his silly head off. That's settled. He eats more than a hired man. I know that. And he tears up everything he can get his teeth into. And he 'runs' the sheep somethin' scand'lous when old Shep and me try to learn him herding. And he hasn't hardly the brains to remember his own name. But—well, a hunch is a hunch. I'm a-going to play mine. Leggy stays."

"Amos Brand!" said his pretty wife, in mock despair. "Nature used up so much wisdom in making Thackeray and Bismarck and Lincoln that she had to strike an average by making two beings that didn't have any wisdom at all. One of them is Leggy. I was dumb enough to marry the other one."

In spite of Ruth's open scorn for his hunch, Amos continued to play it. Not only did he allow the shambling giant collie puppy to continue living at the farm, but he used up an unbelievable store of patience in endless efforts to train Leggy into a semblance of a useful farm dog.

For a month or so longer his attempts were laughably— or cursably—futile. Leggy seemed unable to learn the simplest rudiments of work or of anything else. The pup was good-natured and willing and effusively friendly. But he was a fool.

He ate ravenously; he grew like a weed; he was adoringly fond of everyone he met. But he had not even brains enough to retrieve a thrown stick. Nor to keep from dashing gaily among the driven sheep or cattle, barking and harrying. In vain did Amos Brand labor and belabor. In vain did Shep, the wise little old farm collie, try to teach him by example and by thrashings. Leggy was hopelessly worthless. His master's hunch seemed to have been inspired by a bad-luck demon.

Then came winter. No longer were the cattle and the sheep sent out to the various pastures of the woody hillside farm. They were kept close, during the bitter northland weather. There was scant work for any dog to do. It was the rest season for man and beast, on a thousand farms. Beyond wood-cutting and stock-tending, Amos himself had little to occupy him.

Leggy spent his time eating and dozing or in romping deliriously in the deep snow; or in following the disgusted old Shep from place to place. He looked up to the aged collie with true hero-worship, taking Shep's snubs and thrashings with loving meekness. At last came spring. Long before the cattle were turned out to grass, half of the farm's three hundred sheep were to be sent to pasture on a rocky slope far from the house.

Shep, with no guidance at all from Brand, was wont to take them in charge on such trips; driving them to the rock-pasture with patient precision; and pushing shut the swing-gate behind him. For ten years Shep had done this sort of thing. To him it seemed ridiculously simple. He despised the harum-scarum Leggy for not having the wit to learn such tasks after a hundred teachings.

On this morning Leggy had been shut in the barn when the sheep were driven forth from their fold. Shep was getting a bit rheumatic with age. Brand did not want the old collie's toil to be impeded or redoubled by the pup's scattering of the flock.

Amos's hunch long since had begun to fade. He had decided to get rid of Leggy in the first merciful way that should present itself.

This morning, the flock was unusually hard to drive. For months they had been cooped in the fold. Their memories of being driven—if indeed sheep have sense enough to remember anything at all—were very vague. At every possible chance they would break or wheel back or try to stampede. Shep was kept busy from the moment he set out.

On this first morning Brand went along. Not that he did not trust to Shep's brain and loyalty; but in order to watch the sheep on their entrance to the pasture. Sometimes, very early in the season, the younger ones needed a bit of overseeing, on their initial trip.

Amos frowned in annoyance at the trouble the flock was

giving to Shep, today; and he pitied the plucky efforts of the rheumatic old collie to keep them in formation and moving in the right direction. He frowned more intensely at thought of the worthlessness of Leggy, the pup he had bought to make farm work easier for tired old Shep.

As the procession reached the pasture, the gate was hanging wide. Shep drove his woolly charges straight for it; easing up on his speed, so that they might not jam or break at the gateway.

In spite of his precautions, a six-month wether wheeled in terror at a garter-snake that was sunning itself in the opening. The wether spun around and galloped off at a tangent. Some forty sheep followed.

Shep was about to give chase, when another forty or fifty sheep broke and scattered in a score of directions. Choosing to check this individual scattering, before turning back the first bunch of strays, Shep got into as active motion as his aged bones and sinews could achieve.

It was a heart-breaking task. Brand was heartily sorry for his honest helper. The man was about to join in the rounding-up process when he was aware of a new dog on the scene. At a glance he recognized Leggy. The pup had pried aside a loose board in the ramshackle barn wall and had wiggled through, at a loss of some of his luxuriant coat. Catching the trail, he had followed.

Brand groaned aloud. The situation was bad enough for Shep and himself, without having their work trebled by the aimless barking and charging of this excited pup. He drew in a long breath, to bellow an order to Leggy to come back to him. But the bellow died unborn in his throat.

To Brand's astonishment, Leggy circled the farthest bunch of galloping strays with the skill of a veteran and the speed of an express train. Deftly, brilliantly, he headed and checked them, sweeping them into alignment and driving them unerringly for the pasture gate.

It was a piece of work that would not have disgraced Shep, in the old collie's best days. True, there was a hint of raggedness and of over-vehemence to it; as to the herding maneuvers of most high-spirited young collies. But it was admirably done, in the main. And it served its purpose to perfection.

Through the gateway cantered the driven bunch and out into the field; spreading and, one by one, stopping to nibble the tiny grassblades. Leggy waited only to see they were not going to double back. Then he dashed after the scattered runaways that Shep was struggling to round up.

It was a pretty sight, this swiftly efficient supplementing of the old dog's work. Incredibly soon, the strays were bunched and turned; and were trotting into the field. There, Shep nosed shut the gate, whose bar fell automatically into place.

Then the ancient sheep-dog walked across to where Leggy stood panting and grinning. Never before had Shep approached the puppy, save in castigation. Now, his motheaten tail awag, he touched noses with his young disciple.

In that brief contact, chumship was established and recognition was given to an able fellow craftsman. Leggy wagged his own plumed tail ecstatically at the compliment.

Amos Brand had stood staring, open-mouthed. Yet his common sense told him it was no miracle at all. Leggy had been trained and drilled into this sort of work, month after month. A hundred times he had seen Shep go through the same evolutions. The average pup would have learned long ago. Leggy's newly-awakened brain was just beginning to function.

Brand looked the pup over with new eyes. For months, he scarce had glanced at him. Now he saw a real miracle. The long winter had done more than awaken Leggy's brain. It had filled out his scrawny body to shapely leanness and to breadth of shoulder and depth of chest. It had given him a mighty coat and had chiseled his amorphous head into

Leggy circled the farthest bunch of strays.

strongly classic lines. The silly puppy eyes had grown stern and deeper-set. A soul had been born into them.

No longer was Leggy a formlessly gangling atrocity. He was a well-built young giant with brawn and brain. Such transformations have occurred in a million seemingly hopeless pups. But Brand was witnessing the phenomenon for the first time. Small wonder that he stared agape.

Thus began a new era in Leggy's life. From a despised nuisance, he took now an honored place in the daily routine of the farm. He was busy. But he was splendidly happy. Not only did Amos Brand and Ruth treat him with real affection and grant him the privilege of kitchen and porch; but his idol, Shep, accepted him as a loved equal. The two dogs were more and more close chums; to Leggy's manifest pride and delight. Except when work separated them, they were always together.

Not only with the wethers and older sheep, but presently with the lambs, did Brand trust the young dog. Almost at once the raggedness and the too vehement tendencies disappeared from his herding technique. With the lambs, Leggy was as gentle as a mother with a sick child. The lamb flock was his joy. He tended it indefatigably. Once, when a mongrel stray dog ventured into the lamb-pasture, Leggy thrashed the intruder wellnigh to death.

And so the springtime and early summer wore on. With each passing day, Leggy waxed more efficient. The seemingly thrown-away lessons of earlier months were bearing rich fruit. Amos Brand rejoiced noisily in his hunch's triumph.

Then came the order for thirty of Amos's lambs to be shipped on a certain date to a dealer in Paterson. Brand selected those that were to be sent. He herded them by themselves in a high-fenced little pasture at the corner of his South Mowing. To Leggy was assigned the task of guarding them, during the few nights before shipment. Vastly proud of himself was Leggy at this welcome duty.

But as Amos, with Shep at his heels, was making his early round of the farm, the first morning after he had put the lambs into the little pasture, the man came upon a sight that sickened and amazed him.

Of the thirty lambs, two had disappeared. The others were close huddled in a corner. One of them had a hideously deep gash on its shoulder.

Leggy half-lay, half-sat, guarding the huddled flock of babies. His right foreleg trailed helpless. One of his furry tulip ears was slashed through. He was bleeding freely from a face-cut, just below the mangled ear.

As Brand approached, the young collie reared up and sought to hobble toward him, wagging his plumed tail. The attempt was too much. Pain and loss of blood made him stagger and then collapse on his side.

Amos called his hired man, bidding the astounded worker pick up the stricken dog and carry him to the house; then telephone to the nearest veterinary to come and set the broken leg and tend the other hurts.

Old Shep nosed his injured chum; whimpering softly in sympathy and then trotting along to the house in the wake of the man who was carrying the invalid. But for once Leggy did not respond in any way to his collie comrade's advances. Indeed, he seemed not to notice the solicitous Shep.

Left alone in the pasture, Brand began to study the trampled grass. There had been a light shower, just before dawn. Thus, the ground still held the marks of the wildly pattering lamb hoofs; and many dog footprints. Apparently, the lambs had been scared into galloping panic by their assailant, and Leggy had done much footwork in the course of their defense.

But, apart from these prints, there was nothing on the wet grass to betoken what manner of beast of prey had carried off two of the lambs and torn a third and had disabled Leggy. The thing was an absolute mystery.

Homeward went Brand, carrying the hurt lamb. He found
Leggy installed on a soft folded blanket in the kitchen, with
Ruth bathing his cuts and trying to ease the pain in the broken
foreleg.

Grimly, Amos set to examining the slashed ear and the
deep cut on the face. The wounds might well have been
made with a dull knife.

"I can't figure it out," he told his wife. "Some critter has
come there in the night and gotten away with two lambs, and
bit another one. Leggy must have put up a good fight. But
what critter could have made such a wound as either of these
on him; and what critter could have broke his leg? That's
what I can't work out."

"I don't know about the leg," answered his wife. "But the
first minute I set eyes on the slit ear and the cut on his face,
I got to remembering the fight old Shep had, that time, six
years back, with Connors' big mastiff. Remember how Connors wouldn't believe a lot of dog bites could cut his mastiff
so that the wounds looked like knifeslits? You told him no dog
but a collie knows how to 'slash' like that when he fights.
Even then, he wouldn't believe Shep's eye-teeth had made
those cuts in his Tige's body. He swore you had attacked
the mastiff with a knife, I remember. Well, these wounds
on Leggy are just like those on Tige."

"H'm!" commented Brand. "I don't see that you've cleared
it up very much. Come to think of it, there can't have been
a fight at all. If any collie had been in a fight with Leggy,
there'd be hair and blood on Leggy's jaws. There isn't a mark
on them. I just looked. Of course, if he had had a chance to
get a good big drink of water, the hair and most likely the
blood would have been washed away. But there's no place in
that pasture where he could have drunk. The drinking-trough
is a hundred feet from where he was lying. He couldn't
have got to it. Besides, how about the broken leg?"

"I—I don't know," she answered. "Unless he may have been thrown, in the fight; and the leg may have doubled under him and broken. That would have been possible."

"I tell you there wasn't any fight," insisted Brand. "You saw how he chewed up that big runaway mongrel last month —the one that got into the uphill pasture. Well, do you suppose he'd have let any dog get away without marking him? Not Leggy. His mouth and chest would have blood on them; and there'd be hairs on his jaws. No, there wasn't any fight!"

"What was there, then?"

"There was some critter that either jumped over the fence or shinned in through the bars and yanked away two of the fattest lambs and barked a third one; and had the size and strength to smash Leggy before the poor chap could even get into action. The only trouble with that idea is that there weren't any tracks such as the critter must have made. Nothing but dog footprints and lamb footprints. And I've just showed you that if it was a dog Leggy would have licked him or else he'd have done enough fighting to leave the marks on his own mouth."

"Yes," said Ruth, wearily, "you've showed me that—or you've tried to. But what does it all add up to?"

"I'd give the year's crops to know," replied Amos, despondently. "But there's one thing——"

He was cut short in his disconsolate speech by the arrival of the veterinary. Soon Leggy's fractured foreleg was in a cast, and his head-wounds were stitched and swathed. The leg-break had not occurred near a joint. Wherefore the vet assured Brand that with any sort of luck the collie would recover wholly from the fracture and would not be lamed for life.

The vet was as mystified as were the Brands, as to the cause of the injuries. He agreed with Ruth that the bone might perhaps have been broken, had the leg been doubled under the dog in a heavy fall. But he said the head-cuts had the aspect of knife slashes, rather than marks of rending by teeth.

That night, Amos Brand deputed Shep to guard the lamb pasture. He himself augmented the vigil by going thither with a twelve-gauge gun whose two barrels contained buckshot cartridges.

Brand seated himself on a rock at one end of the small upland field; wrapping his coat around him and holding the gun in readiness across his knees.

Shep lay down at his feet; his alert old eyes on the drowsing lambs; his ears pricked for the faintest sound. The collie seemed to realize that much was at stake, for he was tense all over; nor did he lower his head to his outstretched paws.

For hours the two watchers remained thus, while the solemn summer night rolled along. The air was tinged with the first chill of distant autumn. The earliest katydids were essaying doubtfully and rustily their frost-warning song. Treetoads and crickets swelled the scratchy chorus. But in and around the pasture there was no other sound.

As the night waxed later and colder, the insect songs ceased. An owl in the nearby patch of woodland began to hoot eerily. A rooster, on the farm across the river, sent out a premature challenge to the dawn. The crowing was answered from Brand's chicken-yard.

Then all went silent again. Brand's head began to nod. Shep's did not. Twice or thrice, Amos started guiltily from a half-doze. Presently he slept. The collie alone kept vigil.

Gray daybreak was crawling out of the east and over the far-off mountain wall, when Amos was waked by the discomfort of his own cramped posture. Roosters were crowing. One or two late summer birds were singing in the woods. The whole pasture was visible, in the unearthly gray light. The dawn wind was blowing.

Brand jumped to his feet. Instantly he sat down again, heavily; his numbed legs buckling. As he stamped the circulation back into his feet he peered worriedly around the little field. He had slept when he should have guarded. He was ashamed of his own negligence.

Shep was broad awake, and thumped his ragged tail on the ground in morning greeting to his master. Brand got up and, followed by the dog, made the round of the field. He counted the lambs.

All were there—alive and unhurt. Through no virtue of their owner, they had gone safely through the night. The mysterious prowler had not paid another visit to the pasture.

Relieved, if still ashamed of himself, Brand sat down again. Dawn deepened into daylight. There was a flush of shimmering gold along the line of eastern mountains. The night was over.

"Sun'll be up in another three minutes, Sheppy," said Amos, snapping his fingers to his dog. "No use of sticking around here any longer. Nothing will ever raid, after daylight comes. Let's go back to the house."

He set forth for home. Ten minutes later, as he finished changing his dew-soaked outer clothes, he remembered he had left his gun lying alongside the rock.

Annoyed at his own gross carelessness, he returned to the pasture for the weapon. As he neared the gate, he saw the lambs were huddled, bleating and milling, in the farthest corner of the enclosure.

Amos broke into a run. In another moment he was among the scared animals; hurriedly counting them.

Two were gone.

Brand had not been absent fifteen minutes in all. When he had left, the flock was intact. Now it was two short, in numbers; and the survivors were jostling one another in mortal fear.

None of them, this time, bore wounds. Nor was there any track on the trampled grass, save theirs and his own and Shep's. Yet, in that brief space of time, some intruder had entered the pasture and had carried off two of the best lambs.

Climbing a pasture tree, Amos surveyed the surrounding country. For some distance in every direction the land lay open. Not a sign of any predatory animal was to be seen. He ran to the patch of woodland, and traversed it eagerly. Nothing was there, to guide him to a clue.

"A lamb don't weigh as much as an elephant," he muttered, half-aloud, scratching his head and trying to fight back a feeling of awe. "But it weighs enough to make it a mighty heavy load for any dog or wolf to lug off. No critter could travel fast, toting one of them. But this critter has got away with *two*. Got away so fast that he's out of sight with them, in just these few minutes. Why, a grown man couldn't lug away two live lambs fast enough to have got clean out of sight in that time! It—it isn't possible. But it's happened, just the same. . . . I'll ship that bunch to Paterson tomorrow. I'm not taking any more chances."

Before he went home, he strode to the main sheep-pasture on the rocky hillside beyond. There he made careful count of his flock. None was missing. None seemed frightened.

"I didn't suppose the critter would hurt them," mused Brand, "so long as he could get tender lambs. Lambs are better to eat, and they don't weigh so much to carry off."

Whereat, he turned homeward, to break the newest bad tidings to his wife.

Ruth was not content to let the matter rest so philosophically as was her husband. Nor was she willing to ascribe it vaguely to "some critter." Her frugal soul was stirred to wrath by the wanton destruction of four valuable lambs in two short days.

She had been sitting on the kitchen floor, renewing Leggy's head bandages, when her husband entered. She had grown to love the young dog. She rejoiced that he was doing so well, after his mishap. Indeed, she found it difficult to make Leggy lie still. The cast protected his fractured foreleg. And his youth and energy made him want to be up and about.

He had proved, already, this morning, what many another healthy dog in like plight has proved;—that a strong collie can manipulate his body on three legs, almost as rapidly as on four, for short distances. A dog with a foreleg in a cast *walks* slowly and clumsily. But often he can *run* with great speed; by the great motorforce of his hindquarters.

Leggy had scrambled to his feet and had run forward to greet Ruth on her arrival in the kitchen, much to her horror. She had made him lie down again at once, and she had feared lest the exertion might have injured his leg.

Now, at her husband's news, she forgot all else save their misfortune in losing the four lambs. She plied Amos with questions, none of which he could answer. All he could tell her was that the flock had been safe when he left the field, at daybreak; and that, within a quarter-hour, two of its members had been spirited away, with no trace of their direction left to guide him.

"You say you looked all around?" she queried. "Why, from the top of that tree you could see for pretty near a mile, in every way except the woods. And you looked through those. That proves no animal or man could have taken them. There's just one way they could have gone. You looked too far. They were close by. I know it. It's the only idea that makes sense."

"It don't make sense to *me*," declared Amos. "I don't see what you're driving at."

"No man or beast could have carried two lambs a mile inside of fifteen minutes," she expounded. "You'll grant that. Well, no man or beast tried to. Any strong critter could have carried them the hundred yards or less, to the outbuildings here, in that time. He could have dragged them under the barn or under any other building or into any of a dozen hiding-places."

"But——"

"And that's what he did," she went on, unheeding. "It's as

clear as the hand in front of your wrist. And it's the only answer. I thought it over, yesterday, about the other two that were stolen. This thing, today, makes me sure."

"Sure of *what*?" inquired the puzzled man.

"I had been downstairs here, working over Leggy, two or three minutes this morning, when you came in from the pasture to change your clothes," said Ruth, with seeming irrelevance. "I've been here ever since. So has he. That proves Leggy couldn't have done it, I ——"

"Who in blue blazes ever supposed Leggy did it?" he asked in vexed bewilderment. "What are you driving at?"

"The hired man didn't do it," she resumed, unchecked. "Because he didn't come downstairs, till a minute ago. You and I didn't do it. That leaves just *one* that could have done it. And he's the one that did. I'm talking about Shep."

"Shep?" the man echoed, in blank incredulity. "You're crazy! He ——"

"No, I'm not," she denied. "But Shep is. I've read about cases like that in Dad's veterinary books. Cases where sheep dogs 'go bad,' in their old age."

"Nonsense! Why, Shep is ——"

"Shep is the critter that drug those lambs away and killed them. I know it. The books said such dogs' minds go queer, and they get a sort of craftiness that makes them as clever as a fox in keeping folks from finding them out. There was a sheep dog of Dad's when he was a young man ——"

"I'm telling you it's *you* who's gone queer—you, not Shep!" cried the astonished Brand. "You know as well as I do that Shep couldn't do such a thing as that, to save his life. Besides," he ended, in sorry triumph, "Shep was with me all night long. He was with me till I left the pasture this morning. So he couldn't ——"

"Did he come back to the house with you?" she insisted, answering her own question by adding, "No, he didn't. I saw you come up the walk. You were alone. Here's what Shep did—he stayed behind. The minute your back was turned he grabbed up one of the lambs and he carried it to some hiding-place under the barn or under one of the sheds. He sneaked back and got another one. Then he heard you coming out of the house and he hid. That's what happened."

Unbelieving, puzzled by her logic, Amos stood glowering at his wife. Scarce stopping for breath, she hastened on:

"Dad always said that the wiser a dog was, the craftier killer he became. That's what Shep has done. You figured no wild animal would raid the pasture, so near to the house, by broad daylight. But you didn't count on Shep. The minute he had a chance, he did it. He couldn't kill them in the night, because you were there. Even if he had been left alone on guard with them, he wouldn't have done it. He would have known we'd understand right off that it was he who did it. But he knew you wouldn't expect him to go back to the pasture, after you and he had been watching there together all night and——"

"I tell you," rasped Amos, "Shep would no sooner——"

"The thing that gave me the idea, first," pursued Ruth, "was the looks of these two cuts on Leggy's head. They are just like the slashes on the mastiff that Shep licked six years ago. No dog but a collie slashes like that. The others are only just bite and tear. A collie does those things. But he slashes, too. Just as Leggy is slashed. Leggy was guarding the lamb pasture, night before last. Shep went there to steal those two lambs. Leggy tried to defend them. Shep attacked him and——"

"And Leggy could swallow Shep in two bites," interposed Brand. "He's twice Shep's size, and he's ten years younger. You saw how he can fight, the day he whipped the mongrel, out yonder, last month. Why, he'd have murdered Shep in a fight!"

"I didn't say they fought," argued Ruth. "They didn't. From the first, Leggy has never fought back when Shep has tackled him. He thinks the world of Shep. He stood guard over the lambs; and most likely he wouldn't let Shep get past him. Just stood between Shep and the lambs, like a sort of barrier. That would be Leggy's way, with a dog he loves as he loves Shep. Then Shep sailed into him. In the scrimmage Leggy slipped and fell and his foreleg broke. He was crippled, then, and Shep could steal all the lambs he wanted to. Can't you see? It's as plain as day."

The man listened glumly, striving to make himself believe her claims were absurd. Then he said, turning to the door:

"I'll find out mighty soon. If he's gorging on lambs ——"

"You couldn't find where he's hidden them," she intervened, "without ripping up the flooring of every building that has an air-space under it."

"Maybe not," he agreed. "But if he's been gorging lambs, he'll be bloody; and there'll be wool all over his jaws and ——"

"Unless he's had the craftiness to wash it off. Likely he'd know enough for that. Shep has all the sense there is."

Without reply, Amos made for the porch. There he shouted at the top of his lungs for Shep. Several times he repeated the shout before Shep appeared from around the corner of the barn. The dog was dripping wet. Very evidently he had just returned from a wallow in the orchard brook. In any event, no trace of blood or of wool remained on him.

Long and miserably, Amos Brand surveyed the old dog that had served him so wisely and so loyally for more than ten years. Shep returned his lowering gaze, looking worriedly up into his master's face, his blearing old eyes noting the man's distress.

Then Brand went back into the house. Leggy raised his head from the blanket, wagging his tail in welcome and essaying to jump up. At a sharp word from Amos, the young collie lay back on his couch, but his tail continued to thud the floor, rhythmically.

"I'm going to prove this thing, before I shoot Shep," Amos

told his wife. "And I've figured out how I'll do it. Tonight I'm going to herd those lambs into the barnyard. I'm going to sit up all night watching them. I'm going to have Shep there with me. At daybreak, I'm coming into the house. I want you to be waiting in the back attic window. From there, you can see every inch of the barnyard. You can sit a little way back in the room, so Shep won't know you're there. I'll give you the gun, to have up there with you. You're a better shot, anyhow, than I am. When I come in, watch Shep. If you see him go for a lamb—well ——"

Ruth hesitated. For years, Shep had been a loved and honored member of the Brand household; tenfold earning his keep, and endearing himself much to his master and to his mistress. Yet, in a sheep-raising community there is but one doom for a sheep-killer. Ruth doubted her husband's ability to bring himself to kill the dog that had been his pal for more than a decade.

"Very well," she said, presently. "I'll do it. I'd rather lose one of my fingers or all my teeth. But it has to be done. I—I feel as if somebody in my own family had gone back on us."

At dusk, the remaining lambs were herded by Shep into the barnyard. The bars were put up. Amos Brand seated himself on the fence's top rail and began his night's vigil. Shep lay at his feet. This time, thanks to an afternoon snooze, the man was able to stay awake; though with increasing effort.

Drowsy as he was, Amos dreaded the approach of day; the time when Shep's innocence or guilt must be put to the fearful test. More than once in the darkness, he stooped down and stroked the old collie's bumpy head. At such times Shep would press caressingly against his master's foot and would thump the earth with his scrap of a tail.

Too soon the east began to gray. Amos waited as long as he dared. He knew his wife was watching, gun in hand, behind the open attic window overlooking the barnyard. He felt a foolish impulse to hide Shep somewhere. But he knew the needfully stern code of the sheep-raiser. As the golden light deepened behind the mountains, he got to his feet. He laid his hands remorsefully on his old dog's sagged shoulders. Then he left the yard and went indoors.

As he opened the kitchen door, something flashed out past him—something that ran jerkily, like a kangaroo, yet with much speed. It was Leggy. Wretchedly unhappy at the impending fate of old Shep, Amos let the crippled dog go, unchecked. If Leggy wanted to risk life-lameness by galloping on three legs while the fourth was in a cast, Brand was too concerned over Shep to waste breath in recalling the excited young collie.

The man kicked off his boots, his ears strained and his pulses athrob with miserable anticipation. As he was removing the second boot he heard the sound he had been waiting for.

The sunrise silences were split by the roar of a shotgun.

In his stockinged feet, Amos raced out to the barnyard.

Leggy had gotten up from his blanket that morning at sound of his master's step on the back porch. But as the door opened, it let in a gush of outdoor air which carried on it a faintly elusive odor which made the collie forget Brand's very existence and indeed everything except that he had a death-feud with the creature whose scent he had just caught.

Out toward the barnyard sped Leggy in his awkward three-legged gallop. His hackles were abristle. His teeth were bared.

Ruth Brand, from the attic window, had watched her husband leave the barnyard. She had gripped the gun and held it ready to aim. But, to her secret relief, Shep merely stretched himself, fore and aft, and ambled houseward in Brand's wake. The old dog did not accord so much as a backward glance at the defenseless lambs.

Still holding the gun ready, Ruth waited; on the fool chance the dog would return to the lambs as soon as he should be certain that Amos was not going to come back.

The rising sun sent its first level ray across the farm. On the instant, a huge shadow bulked black against the sun-touched grass. A second shadow swept close behind the first. Ruth looked up to learn the cause of this dual happening.

A bald eagle, fully seven feet from tip to tip, avalanched downward from the upper air. Like a flung stone it swooped.

With the speed of light it dropped among the new-wakened lambs. With the same speed it drove hooked talons into the shoulder fleece of the largest lamb and, with a mighty flapping, began to beat its laden way upward.

Its mate was close behind it, with a like swoop among the bleating lambkins.

Failing to find their prey in the little pasture, and emboldened by the earliness of the hour and by long immunity, the pair of eagles had sighted the flock here, and had come to take their toll. For a week they had dwelt among the crags of the nearer mountains, sallying forth thus at daybreak for their food.

The first eagle had not cleared the ground with its bleating burden when Leggy wriggled his painful way through the bars and was leaping at it. Well did he recall the rank scent of the birds he had sought so valorously and so vainly to fight off from his flock two days before. One of them had lanced his head with its sabre beak. A wing-blow from its mate had ended his battling by breaking his foreleg. The young dog had a score to pay.

If one foreleg was disabled, his hindquarters still had the dynamic power of a racehorse's. Upward he sprang as the bird sought to heave itself and the lamb high enough for soaring flight. Five feet in air Leggy's terrible jaws drove into the eagle's breast-plumage. They drove deep, and they hung on.

It is one thing to bear off a fat little lamb. And it is quite another to sustain the raging weight of a seventy-pound collie. The eagle dropped its ba-a-ing prey. It smote with beak and claw at the dog that had seized it. The collie's weight brought the huge bird to earth, with a crash and a winnowing of pinions.

There, for a moment, dog and eagle battled ferociously.

Leggy had found a grip where he could not well be shaken off. Deep through plumage and skin and flesh his curved white eyeteeth shore their way—and down through the eagle's breastbone.

The bird, meanwhile, was rending with beak and claw; striving to peck out the deep-set eyes; striving to rip the fur-armored young body to shreds with its powerful talons, striving to beat the dog to death with its flapping wings.

The second eagle had wheeled upward from the lamb it was grasping. Now, rushing to its mate's aid, it whizzed down at Leggy in a thunderbolt swoop.

Then it was that Ruth Brand pulled trigger.

It was a ticklish shot; and one that permitted no time for conscious aim. Yet it found its mark. The second eagle crashed into the barnyard, spinning about and flapping convulsively; with two buckshot through its silvery head.

Down it crashed, full atop the two combatants, hammering them to the ground by its weight and its spasmodic jerkings.

As Amos Brand ran into the yard, a bloody figure reared itself out of that ruck of slaughter;—a cut and bleeding collie with his foreleg in a blood-spattered cast. At his feet lay his enemy; fluttering and twisting convulsively, like its mate. The dog's eyetooth had pierced to the eagle's heart; and had ended the wild battle.

"Leggy," crooned Ruth, two hours later, as she sat on the kitchen floor beside the bandage-swathed dog—"Leggy, the doctor says you'll have a few scars, always. But he says you didn't really harm your leg in that awful fight this morning. He says it'll knit nicely. Isn't that wonderful? But"—stretching out her hand, to pat a bumpy old head just within her reach, "you didn't do anything more than Sheppy here would have done if he'd had the chance. Oh, Shep, I'm so ashamed of myself, whenever I look at you!"

The two collies, old and young, lay side by side in the morning sunshine, listening with pleased interest to their wontedly self-contained mistress's praise and crooning. Two tails —one moth-eaten and stumpy, one plumed and luxuriant— thumped the kitchen floor in joyous unison.

JAMES OLIVER CURWOOD

Kazan

Kazan lay mute and motionless, his gray nose between his fore-paws, his eyes half closed. A rock could have appeared scarcely less lifeless than he: not a muscle twitched; not a hair moved; not an eye-lid quivered. Yet every drop of the wild blood in his splendid body was racing in a ferment of excitement that Kazan had never before experienced; every nerve and fiber of his wonderful muscles was tense as steel wire. Quarter-strain wolf, three-quarters "husky," he had lived the four years of his life in the wilderness. He had felt the pangs of starvation. He knew what it meant to freeze. He had listened to the wailing winds of the long Arctic night over the barrens. He had heard the thunder of the torrent and the cataract, and had cowered under the mighty crash of the storm. His throat and sides were scarred by battle, and his eyes were red with the blister of the snows. He was called Kazan, the Wild Dog, because he was a giant among his kind and as fearless, even, as the men who drove him through the perils of a frozen world.

He had never known fear—until now. He had never felt in

him before the desire to *run*—not even on that terrible day in the forest when he had fought and killed the big gray lynx. He did not know what it was that frightened him, but he knew that he was in another world, and that many things in it startled and alarmed him. It was his first glimpse of Civilization. He wished that his master would come back into the strange room where he had left him. It was a room filled with hideous things. There were great human faces on the wall, but they did not move or speak, but stared at him in a way he had never seen people look before. He remembered having looked on a master who lay very quiet and very cold in the snow, and he had set back on his haunches and wailed forth the death song; but these people on the walls looked alive, and yet seemed dead.

Suddenly Kazan lifted his ears a little. He heard steps, then low voices. One of them was his master's voice. But the other —it sent a little tremor through him! Once, so long ago that it must have been in his puppyhood days, he seemed to have had a dream of a laugh that was like the girl's laugh—a laugh that was all at once filled with a wonderful happiness, the thrill of a wonderful love, and a sweetness that made Kazan lift his head as they came in. He looked straight at them, his red eyes gleaming. At once he knew that she must be dear to his master, for his master's arm was about her. In the glow of the light he saw that her hair was very bright, and that there was the color of the crimson *bakneesh* vine in her face and the blue of the *bakneesh* flower in her shining eyes. Suddenly she saw him, and with a little cry darted toward him.

"Stop!" shouted the man. "He's dangerous! Kazan——"

She was on her knees beside him, all fluffy and sweet and beautiful, her eyes shining wonderfully, her hands about to touch him. Should he cringe back? Should he snap? Was she one of the things on the wall, and his enemy? Should he leap at her white throat? He saw the man running forward, pale as death. Then her hand fell upon his head and the touch sent a thrill through him that quivered in every nerve of his body. With both hands she turned up his head. Her face was very close, and he heard her say, almost sobbingly:

"And you are Kazan—dear old Kazan, my Kazan, my hero dog—who brought him home to me when all the others had died! My Kazan—my hero!"

And then, miracle of miracles, her face was crushed down against him, and he felt her sweet, warm touch.

In those moments Kazan did not move. He scarcely breathed. It seemed a long time before the girl lifted her face from him. And when she did, there were tears in her blue eyes, and the man was standing above them, his hands gripped tight, his jaws set.

"I never knew him to let anyone touch him—with their naked hand," he said in a tense, wondering voice. "Move back quietly, Isobel. Good Heaven—look at that!"

Kazan whined softly, his bloodshot eyes on the girl's face. He wanted to feel her hand again; he wanted to touch her face. Would they beat him with a club, he wondered, if he *dared!* He meant no harm now. He would kill for her. He cringed toward her, inch by inch, his eyes never faltering. He heard what the man said—"Good Heaven! Look at that!"— and he shuddered. But no blow fell to drive him back. His cold muzzle touched her filmy dress, and she looked at him, without moving, her wet eyes blazing like stars.

"See!" she whispered. "See!"

Half an inch more—an inch, two inches, and he gave his big gray body a hunch toward her. Now his muzzle travelled slowly upward—over her foot, to her lap, and at last touched the warm little hand that lay there. His eyes were still on her face: he saw a queer throbbing in her bare white throat, and then a trembling of her lips as she looked up at the man with a wonderful look. He, too, knelt down beside them, and put his arm about the girl again, and patted the dog on the head. Kazan did not like the man's touch. He mistrusted it, as nature had taught him to mistrust the touch of all men's hands, but he permitted it because he saw that it in some way pleased the girl.

"Kazan, old boy, you wouldn't hurt her, would you?" said his master softly. "We both love her, don't we, boy? Can't help it, can we? And she's ours, Kazan, all *ours!* She belongs to you and to me, and we're going to take care of her all our lives, and if we ever have to we'll fight for her like hell—won't we? Eh, Kazan, old boy?"

For a long time after they left him where he was lying on the rug, Kazan's eyes did not leave the girl. He watched and listened—and all the time there grew more and more in him the craving to creep up to them and touch the girl's hand, or her dress, or her foot. After a time his master said something, and with a little laugh the girl jumped up and ran to a big, square, shining thing that stood crosswise in a corner, and which had a row of white teeth longer than his own body. He had wondered what those teeth were for. The girl's fingers touched them now, and all the whispering of winds that he had ever heard, all the music of the waterfalls and the rapids and the trilling of birds in springtime, could not equal the sounds they made. It was his first music. For a moment it startled and frightened him, and then he felt the fright pass away and a strange tingling in his body. He wanted to sit back on his haunches and howl, as he had howled at the billion stars in the skies on cold winter nights. But something kept him from doing that. It was the girl. Slowly he began slinking toward her. He felt the eyes of the man upon him, and stopped. Then a little more—inches at a time, with his throat and jaw straight out along the floor! He was half-way to her —half-way across the room—when the wonderful sounds grew very soft and very low.

"Go on!" he heard the man urge in a low, quick voice. "Go on! Don't stop!"

The girl turned her head, saw him cringing there on the

floor, and continued to play. The man was still looking at him, but his eyes could not keep him back now. He went nearer, still nearer, until at last his outreaching muzzle touched her dress where it lay piled on the floor. And then—he lay trembling, for she had begun to sing. He had heard a Cree woman crooning in front of her tepee; he had heard the wild chant of the "Caribou Song"—but he had never heard anything like this wonderful sweetness that fell from the lips of the girl. He forgot his master's presence now. Quietly, cringingly, so that she would not know, he lifted his head. He saw her looking at him; there was something in her wonderful eyes that gave him confidence, and he laid his head in her lap. For the second time he felt the touch of a woman's hand, and he closed his eyes with a long, sighing breath. The music stopped. There came a little fluttering sound above him, like a laugh and a sob in one. He heard his master cough.

"I've always loved the old rascal—but I never thought he'd do that," he said; and his voice sounded queer to Kazan.

II

Wonderful days followed for Kazan. He missed the forests and deep snows. He missed the daily strife of keeping his team-mates in trace, the yapping at his heels, the straight, long pull over the open spaces and the barrens. He missed the "Koosh—koosh—Hoo-yah!" of the driver, the spiteful snap of his twenty-foot caribou-gut whips, and that yelping and straining behind him that told him he had his followers in line. But something had come to take the place of that which he missed. It was in the room, in the air all about him, even when the girl or his master were not near. Wherever she had been, he found the presence of that strange thing that took away his loneliness. It was the woman scent, and sometimes it made him whine softly. He was not lonely, nights, when he should have been out howling at the stars. He was not lonely because one night he prowled about until he found a certain door, and when the girl opened that door in the morning she found him curled up tight against it. She had reached down and hugged him, the thick smother of her long hair falling all over him in a delightful perfume; thereafter she placed a rug before the door for him to sleep upon. All through the long nights he knew that she was just beyond the door, and he was content. Each day he thought less and less of the wild places, and more of her.

Then there came the beginning of the change. There was a strange hurry and excitement around him, and the girl paid less attention to him. He grew uneasy. He sniffed the change in the air, and he began to study his master's face. Then there came the morning, very early, when the *babiche* collar and the iron chain were fastened to him again. Not until he had followed his master out through the door and into the street did he begin to understand. They were sending him away! He sat suddenly back on his haunches and refused to budge.

"Come, Kazan," coaxed the man. "Come on, boy."

He hung back and showed his white fangs. He expected the lash of a whip or the blow of a club, but neither came. His master laughed and took him back to the house. When they left it again, the girl was with them and walked with her hand touching his head. It was she who persuaded him to leap up through a big dark hole into the still darker interior of a car, and it was she who lured him to the darkest corner of all, where his master fastened his chain. Then they went out, laughing like two children. For hours after that, Kazan lay still and tense, listening to the queer rumble of wheels under him. Several times those wheels stopped, and he heard voices outside. At last he was sure that he heard a familiar voice, and he strained at his chain and whined. The closed door slid back. A man climbed in with a lantern, followed by his master. He paid no attention to them, but glared out through the opening into the gloom of night. He almost broke loose when he leaped down upon the white snow, but when he saw no one there, he stood rigid, sniffling the air. Over him were the stars he had howled at all his life, and about him were the forests, black and silent, shutting them in like a wall. Vainly he sought for that one scent that was missing, and Thorpe heard the low note of grief in his shaggy throat. He took the lantern and held it above his head, at the same time loosening his hold on the leash. At that signal there came a voice from out of the night. It came from behind them, and Kazan whirled so suddenly that the loosely held chain slipped from the man's hand. He saw the glow of other lanterns. And then, once more, the voice——

"Kaa-aa-zan!"

He was off like a bolt. Thorpe laughed to himself as he followed.

"The old pirate!" he chuckled.

When he came to the lantern-lighted space back of the caboose, Thorpe found Kazan crouching down at a woman's feet. It was Thorpe's wife. She smiled triumphantly at him as he came up out of the gloom.

"You've won!" he laughed, not unhappily. "I'd have wagered my last dollar he wouldn't do that for any voice on earth. You've won! Kazan, you brute, I've lost you!"

His face suddenly sobered as Isobel stooped to pick up the end of the chain.

"He's yours, Issy," he added quickly, "but you must let me care for him until—*we know*. Give me the chain. I won't trust him even now. He's a wolf. I've seen him take an Indian's hand off at a single snap. I've seen him tear out another dog's jugular in one leap. He's an outlaw—a bad dog—in spite of the fact that he hung to me like a hero and brought me out alive. I can't trust him. Give me the chain——"

He did not finish. With a snarl of a wild beast Kazan had

leaped to his feet. His lips drew up and bared his long fangs. His spine stiffened, and with a sudden cry of warning, Thorpe dropped a hand to the revolver at his belt.

Kazan paid no attention to him. Another form had approached out of the night, and stood now in the circle of illumination made by the lanterns. It was McCready, who was to accompany Thorpe and his young wife back to the Red River camp, where Thorpe was in charge of the building of the new Trans-continental. The man was straight, powerfully built, and clean shaven. His jaw was so square that it was brutal, and there was a glow in his eyes that was almost like the passion in Kazan's as he looked at Isobel.

Her red and white stocking-cap had slipped free of her head and hung over her shoulder. The dull blaze of the lanterns shone in the warm gold of her hair. Her cheeks were flushed, and her eyes, suddenly turned to him, were as blue as the bluest *bakneesh* flower and glowed like diamonds. McCready shifted his gaze, and instantly her hand fell upon Kazan's head. For the first time the dog did not seem to feel her touch. He still snarled at McCready, the rumbling menace in his throat growing deeper. Thorpe's wife tugged at the chain.

"Down, Kazan—down!" she commanded.

At the sound of her voice he relaxed.

"Down!" she repeated, and her free hand fell on his head again. He slunk to her feet. But his lips were still drawn back. Thorpe was watching him. He wondered at the deadly venom that shot from the wolfish eyes, and looked at McCready. The big guide had uncoiled his long dog-whip. A strange look had come into his face. He was staring hard at Kazan. Suddenly he leaned forward, with both hands on his knees, and for a tense moment or two he seemed to forget Isobel Thorpe's wonderful blue eyes were looking at him.

"Hoo-koosh, Pedro—*charge!*"

That one word—*charge*—was taught only to the dogs in the service of the Northwest Mounted Police. Kazan did not move. McCready straightened, and quick as a shot sent the long lash of his whip curling out into the night with a crack like a pistol report.

"Charge, Pedro—*charge!*"

The rumble in Kazan's throat deepened to a snarling growl, but not a muscle of his body moved. McCready turned to Thorpe.

"I could have sworn that I knew that dog," he said. "If it's Pedro he's *bad!*"

Thorpe was taking the chain. Only the girl saw the look that came for an instant into McCready's face. It made her shiver. A few minutes before, when the train had first stopped at Le Pas, she had offered her hand to this man and she had seen the same thing then. But even as she shuddered she recalled the many things her husband had told her of the forest people. She had grown to love them, to admire their big, rough manhood and loyal hearts, before he had brought her among them; and suddenly she smiled at McCready, struggling to overcome that thrill of fear and dislike.

"He doesn't like you." She laughed at him softly. "Won't you make friends with him?"

She drew Kazan toward him, with Thorpe holding the end of the chain. McCready came to her side as she bent over the dog. His back was to Thorpe as he hunched down. Isobel's bowed head was within a foot of his face. He could see the glow in her cheek and the pouting curve of her mouth as she quieted the low rumbling in Kazan's throat. Thorpe stood ready to pull back on the chain, but for a moment McCready was between him and his wife, and he could not see McCready's face. The man's eyes were not on Kazan. He was staring at the girl.

"You're brave," he said. "I don't dare do that. He would take off my hand!"

He took the lantern from Thorpe and led the way to a narrow snow-path branching off from the track. Hidden back in the thick spruce was the camp which Thorpe had left a fortnight before. There were two tents there now in place of the one which he and his guide had used. A big fire was burning in front of them. Close to the fire was a long sledge, and fastened to trees just within the outer circle of firelight Kazan saw the shadowy forms and gleaming eyes of his team-mates. He stood stiff and motionless while Thorpe fastened him to the sledge. Once more he was back in his forests—and in command. His mistress was laughing and clapping her hands delightedly in the excitement of the strange and wonderful life of which she had now become a part. Thorpe had thrown back the flap of their tent, and she was entering ahead of him. She did not look back. She spoke no word to him. He whined, and turned his red eyes on McCready.

In the tent Thorpe was saying:

"I'm sorry old Jackpine wouldn't go back with us, Issy. He drove me down, but for love or money I couldn't get him to return. He's a Mission Indian and I'd give a month's salary to have you see him handle the dogs. I'm not sure about this man McCready. He's a queer chap, the Company's agent here tells me, and knows the woods like a book. But dogs don't like a stranger. Kazan isn't going to take to him worth a cent!"

Kazan heard the girl's voice, and stood rigid and motionless listening to it. He did not hear or see McCready when he came up stealthily behind him. The man's voice came as suddenly as a shot at his heels.

"*Pedro!*"

In an instant Kazan cringed as if touched by a lash.

"Got you that time—didn't I, you old devil!" whispered McCready, his face strangely pale in the firelight. "Changed your name, eh? But I *got* you—didn't I?"

III

For a long time after he had uttered those words McCready sat in silence beside the fire. Only for a moment or two at a time did his eyes leave Kazan. After a little, when he was sure that Thorpe and Isobel had retired for the night, he went into his own tent and returned with a flask of whiskey. During the next half-hour he drank frequently. Then he went over and sat on the end of the sledge, just beyond the reach of Kazan's chain.

"Got you, didn't I?" he repeated, the effect of the liquor beginning to show in the glitter of his eyes. "Wonder who changed your name, Pedro. And how the devil did *he* come by you? Ho, ho, if you could only talk——"

They heard Thorpe's voice inside the tent. It was followed by a low, girlish peal of laughter, and McCready jerked himself erect. His face blazed suddenly red, and he rose to his feet, dropping the flask in his coat pocket. Walking around the fire, he tiptoed cautiously to the shadow of a tree close to the tent and stood there for many minutes listening. His eyes burned with a fiery madness when he returned to the sledge and Kazan. It was midnight before he went into his own tent.

In the warmth of the fire, Kazan's eyes slowly closed. He slumbered uneasily, and his brain was filled with troubled pictures. At times he was fighting, and his jaws snapped. At others he was straining at the end of his chain, with McCready or his mistress just out of reach. He felt the gentle touch of the girl's hand again and heard the wonderful sweetness of her voice as she sang to him and his master, and his body trembled and twitched with the thrills that had filled him that night. And then the picture changed. He was running at the head of a splendid team—six dogs of the Royal Northwest Mounted Police—and his master was calling him Pedro! The scene shifted. They were in camp. His master was young and smooth-faced and he helped from the sledge another man whose hands were fastened in front of him by curious black rings. Again it was later—and he was lying before a great fire. His master was sitting opposite him, with his back to a tent, and as he looked, there came out of the tent the man with the black rings—only now the rings were gone and his hands were free, and in one of them he carried a heavy club. He heard the terrible blow of the club as it fell on his master's head—and the sound of it roused him from his restless sleep.

He sprang to his feet, his spine stiffening and a snarl in his throat. The fire had died down and the camp was in the darker gloom that precedes dawn. Through that gloom Kazan saw McCready. Again he was standing close to the tent of his mistress, and he knew now that this was the man who had worn the black iron rings, and that it was he who had beaten him with whip and club for many long days after he had killed his master. McCready heard the menace in his throat and came back quickly to the fire. He began to whistle and draw the half-burned logs together, and as the fire blazed up afresh he shouted to awaken Thorpe and Isobel. In a few minutes Thorpe appeared at the tent-flap and his wife followed him out. Her loose hair rippled in billows of gold about her shoulders and she sat down on the sledge, close to Kazan, and began brushing it. McCready came up behind her and fumbled among the packages on the sledge. As if by accident one of his hands buried itself for an instant in the rich tresses that flowed down her back. She did not feel the caressing touch of his fingers, and Thorpe's back was toward them. Only Kazan saw the stealthy movement of the hand, the fondling clutch of the fingers in her hair, and the mad passion burning in the eyes of the man. Quicker than a lynx, the dog had leaped the length of his chain across the sledge. McCready sprang back just in time, and as Kazan reached the end of his chain he was jerked back so that his body struck sidewise against the girl. Thorpe had turned in time to see the end of the leap. He believed that Kazan had sprung at Isobel, and in his horror no word or cry escaped his lips as he dragged her from where she had half fallen over the sledge. He saw that she was not hurt, and he reached for his revolver. It was in his holster in the tent. At his feet was McCready's whip, and in the passion of the moment he seized it and sprang upon Kazan. The dog crouched in the snow. He made no move to escape or to attack. Only once in his life could he remember of having received a beating like that which Thorpe inflicted upon him now. But not a whimper or a growl escaped him.

And then, suddenly, his mistress ran forward and caught the whip poised above Thorpe's head.

"Not another blow!" she cried, and something in her voice held him from striking. McCready did not hear what she said then, but a strange look came into Thorpe's eyes, and without a word he followed his wife into their tent.

"Kazan did not leap at me," she whispered, and she was trembling with a sudden excitement. Her face was deathly white. "That man was behind me," she went on, clutching her husband by the arms. "I felt him touch me—and then Kazan sprang. He wouldn't bite *me*. It's the *man!* There's something—wrong——"

She was almost sobbing, and Thorpe drew her close in his arms.

"I hadn't thought before—but it's strange," he said. "Didn't McCready say something about knowing the dog? It's possible. Perhaps he's had Kazan before and abused him in a way that the dog has not forgotten. Tomorrow I'll find out. But until I know—will you promise to keep away from Kazan?"

Isobel gave the promise. When they came out from the tent Kazan lifted his great head. The stinging lash had closed one of his eyes and his mouth was dripping blood. Isobel gave a low sob, but did not go near him. Half blinded, he knew that his mistress had stopped his punishment, and he whined softly, and wagged his thick tail in the snow.

IV

Never had he felt so miserable as through the long, hard hours of the day that followed, when he broke the trail for his team-mates into the north. One of his eyes was closed and filled with stinging fire, and his body was sore from the blows of the caribou lash. But it was not physical pain that gave the sullen droop to his head and robbed his body of that keen, quick alertness of the lead-dog—the commander of his mates. It was his spirit. For the first time in his life, it was broken. McCready had beaten him—long ago; his master had beaten him; and during all this day their voices were fierce and vengeful in his ears. But it was his mistress who hurt him most. She held aloof from him, always beyond the reach of his leash; and when they stopped to rest, and again in camp, she looked at him with strange and wondering eyes, and did not speak. She, too, was ready to beat him. He believed that, and so slunk away from her and crouched on his belly in the snow. With him, a broken spirit meant a broken heart, and that night he lurked in one of the deepest shadows about the campfire and grieved alone. None knew that it was grief—unless it was the girl. She did not move toward him. She did not speak to him. But she watched him closely—and studied him hardest when he was looking at McCready.

Later, after Thorpe and his mistress had gone into their tent, it began to snow, and the effect of the snow upon Mc-Cready puzzled Kazan. The man was restless, and he drank frequently from the flask which he had used the night before. In the firelight his face grew redder and redder, and Kazan could see the strange gleam of his teeth as he gazed at the tent in which his mistress was sleeping. Again and again he went close to the tent, and listened. Twice he heard movement. The last time, it was the sound of Thorpe's deep breathing. Mc-Cready hurried back to the fire and turned his face straight up to the sky. The snow was falling so thickly that when he lowered his face he blinked and wiped his eyes. Then he went out into the gloom and bent low over the trail they had made a few hours before. It was almost obliterated by the falling snow. Another hour and there would be no trail—nothing to tell whoever might pass the next day that they had come this way. By morning it would cover everything, even the fire, if he allowed it to die down. McCready drank again, out in the darkness. Low words of an insane joy burst from his lips. His head was hot with a drunken fire. His heart beat madly, but scarcely more furiously than did Kazan's when the dog saw that McCready was returning *with a club!* The club he placed on end against a tree. Then he took a lantern from the sledge and lighted it. He approached Thorpe's tent-flap, the lantern in his hand.

"Ho, Thorpe—Thorpe!" he called.

There was no answer. He could hear Thorpe breathing. He drew the flap aside a little, and raised his voice.

"Thorpe!"

Still there was no movement inside, and he untied the flap strings and thrust in his lantern. The light flashed on Isobel's golden head nestling against her husband's shoulder, and Mc-Cready stared at it, his eyes burning like red coals, until he saw that Thorpe was awakening. Quickly he dropped the flap and rustled it from the outside.

"Ho, Thorpe!—Thorpe!" he called again.

This time Thorpe replied.

"Hello, McCready—is that you?"

McCready drew the flap back a little, and spoke in a low voice.

"Yes. Can you come out a minute? Something's happening out in the woods. Don't wake up your wife!"

He drew back and waited. A minute later Thorpe came quietly out of the tent. McCready pointed into the thick spruce.

"I'll swear there's some one nosing around the camp," he said. "I'm certain that I saw a man out there a few minutes ago, when I went for a log. It's a good night for stealing dogs. Here—you take the lantern! If I wasn't clean fooled, we'll find a trail in the snow."

He gave Thorpe the lantern and picked up the heavy club. A growl rose in Kazan's throat, but he choked it back. He wanted to snarl forth his warning, to leap at the end of his leash, but he knew that if he did that, they would return and beat him. So he lay still, trembling and shivering, and whining softly. He watched them until they disappeared—and then waited—listened. At last he heard the crunch of snow. He was not surprised to see McCready come back alone. He had expected him to return alone. For he knew what a club meant!

McCready's face was terrible now. It was like a beast's. He was hatless. Kazan slunk deeper in his shadow at the low, horrible laugh that fell from his lips—for the man still held the club. In a moment he dropped that, and approached the tent. He drew back the flap and peered in. Thorpe's wife was sleeping, and as quietly as a cat he entered and hung the lantern on a nail in the tent-pole. His movement did not awaken her, and for a few moments he stood there, staring—staring.

Outside, crouching in the deep shadow, Kazan tried to fathom the meaning of these strange things that were happening. Why had his master and McCready gone out into the forest? Why had not his master returned? It was his master and not McCready, who belonged in that tent. Then why was McCready there? He watched him as he entered, and suddenly the dog was on his feet, his back tense and bristling, his limbs rigid. He saw McCready's huge shadow on the canvas, and a moment later there came a strange, piercing cry. In the wild terror of that cry he recognized *her* voice—and he leaped toward the tent. The leash stopped him, choking the snarl in his throat. He saw the shadows struggling now, and there

He saw shadows struggling.

came cry after cry. She was calling to his master, and with his master's name she was calling *him!*

"*Kazan—Kazan——*"

He leaped again, and was thrown upon his back. A second and a third time he sprang the length of the leash into the night, and the *babiche* cord about his neck cut into his flesh like a knife. He stopped for an instant, gasping for breath. The shadows were still fighting. Now they were upright! Now they were crumpling down! With a fierce snarl he flung his whole weight once more at the end of the chain. There was a snap, as the thong about his neck gave way.

In half a dozen bounds Kazan made the tent and rushed under the flap. With a snarl he was at McCready's throat. The first snap of his powerful jaws was death, but he did not know that. He knew only that his mistress was there, and that he was fighting for her. There came one choking, gasping cry that ended with a terrible sob; it was McCready. The man sank from his knees upon his back, and Kazan thrust his fangs deeper into his enemy's throat; he felt the warm blood.

The dog's mistress was calling to him now. She was pulling at his shaggy neck. But he would not loose his hold—not for a long time. When he did his mistress looked down once upon the man and covered her face with her hands. Then she sank down upon the blankets. She was very still. Her face and hands were cold, and Kazan muzzled them tenderly. Her eyes were closed. He snuggled up close against her, with his ready jaws turned toward the dead man. Why was she so still, he wondered?

A long time passed, and then she moved. Her eyes opened. Her hand touched him.

Then he heard a step outside.

It was his master, and with that old thrill of fear—fear of the club—he went swiftly to the door. Yes, there was his master in the firelight—and in his hand he held the club. He was coming slowly, almost falling at each step, and his face was red with blood. But he had *the club!* He would beat him again—beat him terribly for hurting McCready; so Kazan slipped quietly under the tent-flap and stole off into the shadows. From out of the gloom of the thick spruce he looked back, and a low whine of love and grief rose and died softly in his throat. They would beat him always now—after *that.* Even *she* would beat him. They would hunt him down, and beat him when they found him.

From out the glow of the fire he turned his wolfish head to the depths of the forest. There were no clubs or stinging lashes out in that gloom. They would never find him there.

For another moment he wavered. And then, as silently as one of the wild creatures of which he was a part, he stole away into the blackness of the night.

JACK LONDON

That Spot

I DON'T think much of Stephen Mackaye any more, though I used to swear by him. I know that in those days I loved him more than my own brother. If ever I meet Stephen Mackaye again, I shall not be responsible for my actions. It passes beyond me that a man with whom I shared food and blanket, and with whom I mushed over the Chilcoot Trail, should turn out the way he did. I always sized Steve up as a square man, a kindly comrade, without an iota of anything vindictive or malicious in his nature. I shall never trust my judgment in men again. Why, I nursed that man through typhoid fever; we starved together on the headwaters of the Stewart; and he saved my life on the Little Salmon. And now, after the years we were together, all I can say of Stephen Mackaye is that he is the meanest man I ever knew.

We started for the Klondike in the fall rush of 1897, and we started too late to get over Chilcoot Pass before the freeze-up. We packed our outfit on our backs part way over, when the snow began to fly, and then we had to buy dogs in order to sled it the rest of the way. That was how we came to get that Spot. Dogs were high, and we paid one hundred and ten dollars for him. He looked worth it. I say *looked*, because he was one of the finest-appearing dogs I ever saw. He weighed sixty pounds, and he had all the lines of a good sled animal. We never could make out his breed. He wasn't husky, nor Malemute, nor Hudson Bay; he looked like all of them and he didn't look like any of them; and on top of it all he had some of the white man's dog in him, for on one side, in the thick of the mixed yellow-brown-red-and-dirty-white that was his prevailing color, there was a spot of coal-black as big as a water-bucket. That was why we called him Spot.

He was a good looker all right. When he was in condition his muscles stood out in bunches all over him. And he was the strongest-looking brute I ever saw in Alaska, also the most intelligent-looking. To run your eyes over him, you'd think he could outpull three dogs of his own weight. Maybe he could, but I never saw it. His intelligence didn't run that way. He could steal and forage to perfection; he had an instinct that was positively grewsome for divining when work was to be done and for making a sneak accordingly; and for getting lost and not staying lost he was nothing short of inspired. But when it came to work, the way that intelligence dribbled out of him and left him a mere clot of wobbling, stupid jelly would make your heart bleed.

There are times when I think it wasn't stupidity. Maybe, like some men I know, he was too wise to work. I shouldn't wonder if he put it all over us with that intelligence of his. Maybe he figured it all out and decided that a licking now and again and no work was a whole lot better than work all the time and no licking. He was intelligent enough for such a computation. I tell you, I've sat and looked into that dog's eyes till the shivers ran up and down my spine and the marrow crawled like yeast, what of the intelligence I saw shining out. I can't express myself about that intelligence. It is beyond mere words. I saw it, that's all. At times it was like gazing into a human soul, to look into his eyes; and what I saw there frightened me and started all sorts of ideas in my own mind of reincarnation and all the rest. I tell you I sensed something big in that brute's eyes; there was a message there, but I wasn't big enough myself to catch it. Whatever it was (I know I'm making a fool of myself)—whatever it was, it baffled me. I can't give an inkling of what I saw in that brute's eyes; it wasn't light, it wasn't color; it was something that moved, away back, when the eyes themselves weren't moving. And I guess I didn't see it move, either; I only sensed that it moved. It was an expression,—that's what it was,—and I got an impression of it. No; it was different from a mere expression; it was more than that. I don't know what it was, but it gave me a feeling of kinship just the same. Oh, no, not sentimental kinship. It was, rather, a kinship of equality. Those eyes never pleaded like a deer's eyes. They challenged. No, it wasn't defiance. It was just a calm assumption of equality. And I don't think it was deliberate. My belief is that it was unconscious on his part. It was there because it was there, and it couldn't help shining out. No, I don't mean shine. It didn't shine; it *moved*. I know I'm talking rot, but if you'd looked into that animal's eyes the way I have, you'd understand. Steve was affected the same way I was. Why, I tried to kill that Spot once—he was no good for anything; and I fell down on it. I led him out into the brush, and he came along slow and unwilling. He knew what was going on. I stopped in a likely place, put my foot on the rope, and pulled my big Colt's. And that dog sat down and looked at me. I tell you he didn't plead. He just looked. And I saw all kinds of incomprehensible things moving, yes, *moving*, in those eyes of his. I didn't really see them move; I thought I saw them, for, as I said before, I guess I only sensed them. And I want to tell you right now that it got beyond me. It was like killing a man, a conscious, brave man who looked calmly into your gun as much as to say, "Who's afraid?" Then, too, the message seemed so near that, instead of pulling the trigger quick, I stopped to see if I could catch the message. There it was, right before me, glimmering all around in those eyes of his. And then it was too late. I got scared. I was trembly all over, and my stomach generated a nervous palpitation that made me seasick. I just sat down and looked at that dog, and he looked at me, till I thought I was going crazy. Do you want to know what I did? I threw down the gun and ran back to camp with the fear of God in my heart. Steve laughed at me. But I notice that Steve led Spot into the woods, a week later, for the same purpose, and that Steve came back alone, and a little later Spot drifted back, too.

At any rate, Spot wouldn't work. We paid a hundred and ten dollars for him from the bottom of our sack, and he wouldn't work. He wouldn't even tighten the traces. Steve spoke to him the first time we put him in harness, and he sort of shivered, that was all. Not an ounce on the traces. He just stood still and wobbled, like so much jelly. Steve touched him with the whip. He yelped, but not an ounce. Steve touched him again, a bit harder, and he howled—the regular long wolf howl. Then Steve got mad and gave him half a dozen, and I came on the run from the tent.

I told Steve he was brutal with the animal, and we had some words—the first we'd ever had. He threw the whip down in the snow and walked away mad. I picked it up and went to it. That Spot trembled and wobbled and cowered before ever I swung the lash, and with the first bite of it he howled like a lost soul. Next he lay down in the snow. I started the rest of the dogs, and they dragged him along while I threw the whip into him. He rolled over on his back and bumped along, his four legs waving in the air, himself howling as though he was going through a sausage machine. Steve came back and laughed at me, and I apologized for what I'd said.

There was no getting any work out of that Spot; and to make up for it, he was the biggest pig-glutton of a dog I ever saw. On top of that, he was the cleverest thief. There was no circumventing him. Many a breakfast we went without our bacon because Spot had been there first. And it was because of him that we nearly starved to death up the Stewart. He figured out the way to break into our meat-cache, and what he didn't eat, the rest of the team did. But he was impartial. He stole from everybody. He was a restless dog, always very busy snooping around or going somewhere. And there was never a camp within five miles that he didn't raid. The worst of it was that they always came back on us to pay his board bill, which was just, being the law of the land; but it was mighty hard on us, especially that first winter on the Chilcoot, when we were busted, paying for whole hams and sides of bacon that we never ate. He could fight, too, that Spot. He could do everything but work. He never pulled a pound, but he was the boss of the whole team. The way he made those dogs stand around was an education. He bullied them, and there was always one or more of them fresh-marked with his fangs. But he was more than a bully. He wasn't afraid of anything that walked on four legs; and I've seen him march, single-handed, into a strange team, without any provocation whatever, and put the *kibosh* on the whole outfit. Did I say he could eat? I caught him eating the whip once. That's straight. He started in at the lash, and when I caught him he was down to the handle, and still going.

But he was a good looker. At the end of the first week we sold him for seventy-five dollars to the Mounted Police. They had experienced dog-drivers, and we knew that by the time he'd covered the six hundred miles to Dawson he'd be a good sled-dog. I say we *knew,* for we were just getting acquainted with that Spot. A little later we were not brash enough to know anything where he was concerned. A week later we woke up in the morning to the dangdest dog-fight we'd ever heard. It was that Spot come back and knocking the team into shape. We ate a pretty depressing breakfast, I can tell you;

but cheered up two hours afterward when we sold him to an official courier, bound in to Dawson with government despatches. That Spot was only three days in coming back, and, as usual, celebrated his arrival with a rough-house.

We spent the winter and spring, after our own outfit was across the pass, freighting other people's outfits; and we made a fat stake. Also, we made money out of Spot. If we sold him once, we sold him twenty times. He always came back, and no one asked for their money. We didn't want the money. We'd have paid handsomely for any one to take him off our hands for keeps. We had to get rid of him, and we couldn't give him away, for that would have been suspicious. But he was such a fine looker that we never had any difficulty in selling him. "Unbroke," we'd say, and they'd pay any old price for him. We sold him as low as twenty-five dollars, and once we got a hundred and fifty for him. That particular party returned him in person, refused to take his money back, and the way he abused us was something awful. He said it was cheap at the price to tell us what he thought of us; and we felt he was so justified that we never talked back. But to this day I've never quite regained all the old self-respect that was mine before that man talked to me.

When the ice cleared out of the lakes and river, we put our outfit in a Lake Bennett boat and started for Dawson. We had a good team of dogs, and of course we piled them on top the outfit. That Spot was along—there was no losing him; and a dozen times, the first day, he knocked one or another of the dogs overboard in the course of fighting with them. It was close quarters, and he didn't like being crowded.

"What that dog needs is space," Steve said the second day. "Let's maroon him."

We did, running the boat in at Caribou Crossing for him to jump ashore. Two of the other dogs, good dogs, followed him; and we lost two whole days trying to find them. We never saw those two dogs again; but the quietness and relief we enjoyed made us decide, like the man who refused his hundred and fifty, that it was cheap at the price. For the first time in months Steve and I laughed and whistled and sang. We were as happy as clams. The dark days were over. The nightmare had been lifted. That Spot was gone.

Three weeks later, one morning, Steve and I were standing on the river-bank at Dawson. A small boat was just arriving from Lake Bennett. I saw Steve give a start, and heard him say something that was not nice and that was not under his breath. Then I looked; and there, in the bow of the boat, with ears pricked up, sat Spot. Steve and I sneaked immediately, like beaten curs, like cowards, like absconders from justice. It was this last that the lieutenant of police thought when he saw us sneaking. He surmised that there were law-officers in the boat who were after us. He didn't wait to find out, but kept us in sight, and in the M. & M. saloon got us in a corner. We had a merry time explaining, for we refused to go back to the boat and meet Spot; and finally he held us under guard of another policeman while he went to the boat. After we got clear of him, we started for the cabin, and when we arrived, there was that Spot sitting on the stoop waiting for us. Now how did he know we lived there? There were forty thousand people in Dawson that summer, and how did he *savve* our cabin out of all the cabins? How did he know we were in Dawson, anyway? I leave it to you. But don't forget what I have said about his intelligence and that immortal something I have seen glimmering in his eyes.

There was no getting rid of him any more. There were too many people in Dawson who had bought him up on Chilcoot, and the story got around. Half a dozen times we put him on board steamboats going down the Yukon; but he merely went ashore at the first landing and trotted back up the bank. We couldn't sell him, we couldn't kill him (both Steve and I had tried), and nobody else was able to kill him. He bore a charmed life. I've seen him go down in a dog-fight on the main street with fifty dogs on top of him, and when they were separated, he'd appear on all his four legs, unharmed, while two of the dogs that had been on top of him would be lying dead.

I saw him steal a chunk of moose-meat from Major Dinwiddie's cache so heavy that he could just keep one jump ahead of Mrs. Dinwiddie's squaw cook, who was after him with an axe. As he went up the hill, after the squaw gave up, Major Dinwiddie himself came out and pumped his Winchester into the landscape. He emptied his magazine twice, and never touched that Spot. Then a policeman came along and arrested him for discharging firearms inside the city limits. Major Dinwiddie paid his fine, and Steve and I paid him for the moose-meat at the rate of a dollar a pound, bones and all. That was what he paid for it. Meat was high that year.

I am only telling what I saw with my own eyes. And now I'll tell you something, also. I saw that Spot fall through a water-hole. The ice was three and a half feet thick, and the current sucked him under like a straw. Three hundred yards below was the big water-hole used by the hospital. Spot crawled out of the hospital water-hole, licked off the water, bit out the ice that had formed between his toes, trotted up the bank, and whipped a big Newfoundland belonging to the Gold Commissioner.

In the fall of 1898, Steve and I poled up the Yukon on the last water, bound for Stewart River. We took the dogs along, all except Spot. We figured we'd been feeding him long enough. He'd cost us more time and trouble and money and grub than we'd got by selling him on the Chilcoot—especially grub. So Steve and I tied him down in the cabin and pulled our freight. We camped that night at the mouth of Indian River, and Steve and I were pretty facetious over having shaken him. Steve was a funny cuss, and I was just sitting up in the blankets and laughing when a tornado hit camp. The way that Spot walked into those dogs and gave them what-for was hair-raising. Now how did he get loose? It's up to you. I haven't any theory. And how did he get across the Klondike River? That's another facer. And anyway, how did he know we had gone up the Yukon? You see, we went by water, and he couldn't smell our tracks. Steve and I began to get superstitious about that dog. He got on our nerves, too; and, between you and me, we were just a mite afraid of him.

The freeze-up came on when we were at the mouth of Henderson Creek, and we traded him off for two sacks of flour to an outfit that was bound up White River after copper. Now that whole outfit was lost. Never trace nor hide nor hair of men, dogs, sleds, or anything was ever found. They dropped clean out of sight. It became one of the mysteries of the country. Steve and I plugged away up the Stewart, and six weeks afterward that Spot crawled into camp. He was a perambulating skeleton, and could just drag along; but he got there. And what I want to know is who told him we were up the Stewart? We could have gone a thousand other places. How did he know? You tell me, and I'll tell you.

No losing him. At the Mayo he started a row with an Indian dog. The buck who owned the dog took a swing at Spot with an axe, missed him, and killed his own dog. Talk about magic and turning bullets aside—I, for one, consider it a blamed sight harder to turn an axe aside with a big buck at the other end of it. And I saw him do it with my own eyes. That buck didn't want to kill his own dog. You've got to show me.

I told you about Spot breaking into our meat-cache. It was nearly the death of us. There wasn't any more meat to be killed, and meat was all we had to live on. The moose had gone back several hundred miles and the Indians with them. There we were. Spring was on, and we had to wait for the river to break. We got pretty thin before we decided to eat the dogs, and we decided to eat Spot first. Do you know what that dog did? He sneaked. Now how did he know our minds were made up to eat him? We sat up nights laying for him, but he never came back, and we ate the other dogs. We ate the whole team.

And now for the sequel. You know what it is when a big river breaks up and a few billion tons of ice go out, jamming and milling and grinding. Just in the thick of it, when the Stewart went out, rumbling and roaring, we sighted Spot out in the middle. He'd got caught as he was trying to cross up above somewhere. Steve and I yelled and shouted and ran up and down the bank, tossing our hats in the air. Sometimes we'd stop and hug each other, we were that boisterous, for we saw Spot's finish. He didn't have a chance in a million. He didn't have any chance at all. After the ice-run, we got into a canoe and paddled down to the Yukon, and down the Yukon to Dawson, stopping to feed up for a week at the cabins at the mouth of Henderson Creek. And as we came in to the bank at Dawson, there sat that Spot, waiting for us, his ears pricked up, his tail wagging, his mouth smiling, extending a hearty welcome to us. Now how did he get out of that ice? How did he know we were coming to Dawson, to the very hour and minute, to be out there on the bank waiting for us?

The more I think of that Spot, the more I am convinced that there are things in this world that go beyond science. On no scientific grounds can that Spot be explained. It's psychic phenomena, or mysticism, or something of that sort, I guess, with a lot of Theosophy thrown in. The Klondike is a good country. I might have been there yet, and become a millionnaire, if it hadn't been for Spot. He got on my nerves. I stood him for two years all together, and then I guess my stamina broke. It was the summer of 1899 when I pulled out. I didn't say anything to Steve. I just sneaked. But I fixed it up all right. I wrote Steve a note, and enclosed a package of "rough-on-rats," telling him what to do with it. I was worn down to skin and bone by that Spot, and I was that nervous that I'd jump and look around when there wasn't anybody within hailing distance. But it was astonishing the way I recuperated when I got quit of him. I got back twenty pounds before I arrived in San Francisco, and by the time I'd crossed the ferry to Oakland I was my old self again, so that even my wife looked in vain for any change in me.

Steve wrote to me once, and his letter seemed irritated. He took it kind of hard because I'd left him with Spot. Also, he said he'd used the "rough-on-rats," per directions, and that there was nothing doing. A year went by. I was back in the office and prospering in all ways—even getting a bit fat. And then Steve arrived. He didn't look me up. I read his name in the steamer list, and wondered why. But I didn't wonder long. I got up one morning and found that Spot chained to the gate-post and holding up the milkman. Steve went north to Seattle, I learned, that very morning. I didn't put on any more weight. My wife made me buy him a collar and tag, and within an hour he showed his gratitude by killing her pet Persian cat. There is no getting rid of that Spot. He will be with me until I die, for he'll never die. My appetite is not so good since he arrived, and my wife says I am looking peaked. Last night that Spot got into Mr. Harvey's hen-house (Harvey is my next door neighbor) and killed nineteen of his fancy-bred chickens. I shall have to pay for them. My neighbors on the other side quarrelled with my wife and then moved out. Spot was the cause of it. And that is why I am disappointed in Stephen Mackaye. I had no idea he was so mean a man.

COREY FORD

Slipstream

He could hear them sometimes in his sleep. They would pass right over the house, taking off from Hinman Field nearby, and his paws would begin to twitch, and as the sound of the engines grew louder his toenails would scratch faster and faster on the hardwood floor and he would make an eager whimpering noise in his throat. And then for a moment the roar overhead would seem to shake the entire house, and he would lift his head suddenly, and open his eyes, and stare emptily at the darkness as they faded away and away into the night.

He had lived all his life within the sound of airplane engines. He had first seen the light of day, one of six squirming pups, in an empty ammo box in the crew chief's shack down on the line. His mother was a collie and belonged to the crew-chief, who always insisted she was part full-blooded. He never saw his father, but he must have been a Pomeranian of some kind, because he alone of the litter was born with pointed ears and a great ruff of fur around his neck, and short stubby legs which persisted in flying in all directions and

66

dumping him on his nose when he tried to run. The chief decided to name him Slipstream.

"Slips for short," he told Bill Bentley, "after his mother's getting mixed up with one of them native dogs. You said you wanted a mascot, Lieutenant."

He got his first airplane ride when he was six weeks old. He took it all in stride, sleeping comfortably on Bill Bentley's folded B-10 jacket until they hit an air-pocket and he found himself two feet above the floor, clawing at space and wetting all over the cockpit. Thereafter Bill always strapped him down in rough air, or when they were on a combat-mission together. He flew quite a few missions with Bill. "It's safer than back at the base," Bill said. "He might get run over by a truck or something." He even got the D.F.C., when Bill's airplane picked up a flak-hole in the fuel line, on the way back from Formosa, and Bill went over the side with Slips clasped firmly under one arm. When they were picked up an hour later, Slips was sitting in the inflated rubber raft and Bill was paddling alone in the water, clinging to the side. Some of the maintenance men made him a leather collar with his name spelled out in copper rivets and an imitation Flying Cross hanging from a metal ring, and the Colonel presented it to him in a formal ceremony one afternoon after mess.

The sound of airplane engines would always bring back those long steamy afternoons, and the smell of cigars and hairtonic and shoe-dubbing and sweat, and the shuffle and snap of playing-cards in the hot Quonset hut. He owned the Quonset, of course. He would burst through the door and scamper heedlessly down the line of cots, leaping from naked chest to naked chest, leaving a wake of cursing pilots and scattered poker-hands and beer-cans upset on blankets as he made a final spring and landed on the table where Bill was writing a letter home to his wife. "Excuse the blots, Helen, Slips just upset the inkwell." He wrote her every day, and he always mentioned Slips. "Dear Helen, This letter will have to be short, Slips chewed up all the writing-paper. . . ." "Slips sends his love, darling, he's promised to look out for you if anything ever happens. . . ."

Or sometimes, at night, the drone of the engines would recall another afternoon when he lay curled on a folded parachute in the ready-room, waiting for Bill to get back from a mission he was flying alone. Waiting and waiting, long after the rest of the squadron had landed again and shuffled past him in heavy flying-gear, their eyes lowered. Waiting until Larry Hollis, who flew on Bill's wing, picked him up in silence and carried him back to the Quonset. Some of the other fliers were gathering up Bill's things and putting them into Bill's blue barracks-bag, and he growled at them uneasily, and Larry patted him a moment and put him on Bill's cot, and sat down heavily at the table and reached for Bill's writing-pad.

"Dear Mrs. Bentley," he began, and crumpled the sheet of paper in his fist, and began again: "Dear Helen. . . ."

He had never been quite sure whether Helen liked him. She never laughed at him, or rumpled his ears, or rolled him over and scratched his belly the way Bill did, and now and then he even had the feeling she resented his being there at all. He had felt it the first time he saw her, the night that Larry carried him up the front steps and rang the doorbell. He was dirty and rumpled after flying two days and nights across the Pacific, and his fur was matted with grease and smelt of high-octane gas and creosote from the floor of the cargo-plane, and his feet had skidded awkwardly on the polished floor of the small clean living room as Larry set him down. "This is Slips. Bill wanted you to have him, Helen. I hope you don't mind my calling you Helen, but I was Bill's best friend. . . ."

He had wagged his tail and looked into her face expectantly, but she was not looking at him. She was all in black, with her hair pulled back from her white face, and her hands were gripped tight. Her eyes were on Larry. "I want you to tell me frankly, Lieutenant. Is there any hope at all?"

Larry shook his head slowly. "I saw it happen."

The room was full of Bill. There were pictures of Bill in his cadet cap, and Bill in flying-helmet and earphones leaning out of the cockpit of his airplane, and Bill's engraved commission, and in an easel-frame on the table was a colored photograph of Bill, wearing his shiny new second lieutenant's bars, beside Helen in a white wedding-dress.

"We were married at Lakenan Field, the night he graduated." She spoke in a flat monotone, as though she were talking in her sleep. "Then he was transferred here to Hinman, and we bought this house, and two days after we moved in he got his assignment overseas. I only had him such a little while. Such a little while."

"I'm stationed at Hinman now," Larry said. "Training program. I wish I could call you up sometime. . . ."

"Thank you, Lieutenant," she said in a dull voice, "but I don't go out much."

Mostly she stayed in her room, reading or knitting or listening to the radio. The phone used to ring at first, but she always gave the same answer, and after a few weeks it stopped ringing. Slips moved aimlessly from room to room, feeling unwanted and alone. All the pictures of Bill in uniform disappeared, the day after he arrived; there was only a snapshot, taken when Bill was in college, on the living-room table. Even his leather collar with the Flying Cross disappeared, the first time that Helen gave him a bath and washed away the lingering airplane-aroma of gasoline and grease. He had crawled under the sofa after his bath, licking off the scented soap and shivering at the strange sweet way he smelled. He never saw his collar again.

Larry Hollis came to see him once. He barked at the unexpected peal of the doorbell, and then, as he saw in the doorway the polished jodhpur boots and the pinks and the green Army blouse and combat ribbons, he howled and raced toward him and leapt up into his arms, wriggling, frantically lapping his chin and neck. Larry laughed and scratched his ruff and put him down, and he leapt back into his arms again, bowling him backward into a chair. He curled up on his lap and lay still, resting his muzzle against the cool silver wings on Larry's blouse, trying to stop whimpering. Larry looked around him at the bare walls, and at the solitary photograph on the table. "It's funny, you know, but I never saw Bill in civilian clothes."

"I never did, either," Helen said bitterly. "His mother sent it to me. It's the only picture I have of him that doesn't remind me of . . ." She let the sentence die.

Larry fished in his pocket for a paper. "They've just awarded him the Silver Star. I thought maybe you'd like to have the citation."

Helen took it without reading it, and put it on the table. Her face was thinner and older, Larry saw, and her eyes seemed to be fixed on something far away. He fumbled for a cigarette.

"Look, Helen." He flicked a lighter. "Maybe I haven't got any right to say this, but . . ." He lit the cigarette, snapped the lighter shut. "They're having a little dance Saturday at the Field. Wouldn't it be a good thing if you—I mean, got out and saw people again? I mean, after all, Bill wouldn't want you to be like this."

"Thank you, Lieutenant." Her face was a mask. "You're very thoughtful, but . . . I'm afraid I wouldn't be much fun."

Slips could find no way of getting behind that mask. He tagged after her wherever she went, but she did not seem to notice him; she ignored the old glove he brought her to throw for him; when he put his paws on her knee, she pushed him down. She never smiled; he could not make her smile. He slid clownishly on the scatter-rugs for her approval; he pretended to hear mice; he put on a great act one day with an ant he discovered on the living-room floor, but she sat rocking in her chair by the window, and at last he abandoned the ant and walked disconsolately down the hall and into the bedroom. The closet door was open; he had never seen it unlocked before. He poked his head inside, and sniffed. A wonderful remembered smell greeted his nostrils. He craned his neck toward a bulky shape at the back of the closet, inhaling deeply, beginning to pant with eagerness. Some boxes stood in front of it; he braced his paws on them and tugged at a dangling cord, until the blue barracks-bag toppled toward him, opening as it fell and spilling out a rusted razor and Bill's fountain-pen and the framed picture of Helen that had stood on the table beside his cot. The bag was wadded full of moldy flying clothes and he burrowed deeper into it in a frenzy of excitement, pulling out a musty B-10 jacket, a pair of fleece-lined boots tied together by their zippers, Bill's crumpled flight-cap—his thousand-hour hat, he always called it—with the sweat-stained vizor and the brass emblem bent and tarnished.

Helen looked up as he trotted proudly across the living-room floor toward her, holding the vizor in his teeth. She caught her breath with a sharp sob, snatched the cap out of his mouth, and slapped him across the muzzle with it, twice. Her sobbing frightened him so that he forgot to yelp when he was hit. She whirled and ran blindly out of the room, slamming the bedroom door behind her, and a moment later the key turned in the closet door, and he heard the creak of springs as she flung herself on the bed.

He pushed the screen-door open with his nose, and slunk out onto the front porch. There was a drone of airplane engines in the distant sky, and he looked up at a pair of red and green lights moving slowly across the stationary stars. It was no use; he was not wanted here. He walked down the steps, and through the front gate and down the street, following the sound of engines fading into the night. . . .

The Sergeant saw him first, as he limped across the hard-surfaced runway late the following afternoon. "G'on," he yelled at him, "beat it." The pads of his feet were worn raw, and his tongue lagged as he made his way slowly toward the group of men working around an airplane on the parking-area. "You're a hell of a lookin' pooch," the Sergeant grumbled. He was too tired to trot; his head hung low, swaying from side to side, and his glassy eyes were fixed ahead. He dropped on his belly in front of a pair of heavy Army shoes. "He's hungry, Sarge," one of the mechanics said. "Let's take him over to the mess-hall and get him somepin' to eat."

The warm steamy mess-hall; clatter of tin, rumble of masculine voices, the gleam of sweaty bodies behind the counter; the men in oil-stained coveralls straddling the board plank alongside the mess-table, handing him chunks of bread, pieces of meat; the big calloused hand, smelling of gasoline, that reached down now and then to rough his fur. "Who the hell's dog is it?" someone asked. "I seen him first," the Sergeant said belligerently, "he's mine."

They started back across the field, his well-filled belly as round as a football under the Sergeant's shaggy forearm. Larry Hollis, approaching the mess-hall, halted in astonishment.

"Isn't that . . . Sure it is. Hey, Slips!" He dropped from the Sergeant's grasp and ran eagerly toward Larry, leaping up at him. "How in all hell did you get here?" Larry gasped.

"I'm sorry, sir," the Sergeant said. "I didn't know it was anybody's dog."

"It's all right, Sergeant. Take him back to your quarters, and just keep an eye on him. I've got to make a phone-call. . . ."

Helen's car sounded its horn in front of the barracks, and the Sergeant opened the door. He saluted Larry. "The dog's right here, sir," he said. "I'll get him."

Over the Sergeant's shoulder, Helen could see the long aisle, the men sprawled asleep on the double row of cots, the bare backs of a group of poker-players around a table at the end of the room. Slips jumped off a cot obediently, at the Sergeant's whistle, and trotted through the door. He saw Helen, and his pace slowed to a walk. He came toward her dutifully, his ears down.

"Slips," she cried, sweeping him up in her arms and holding him tight, her cheek pressed against his fur. She had never hugged him before. "Oh, Slips."

"I'll put him in the car," Larry offered.

"No, Larry," she said, still hugging Slips. "I . . . I'm leaving him here. It isn't right for him to be all alone."

"It isn't right for anybody to be all alone," Larry said in a low voice. He hesitated. "That dance I was telling you about. It's tonight."

She put Slips down. He looked up at her, and at Larry, and then, as though he were satisfied his job was done, he turned and dashed back into the barracks, hopping onto the end cot and leaping joyously from chest to chest across the sleeping figures until, with a final spring, he landed in the center of the poker game. Cards scattered, a chorus of curses arose, the Sergeant hurriedly slammed the door.

Larry was looking at Helen. It was the first time he had ever seen her laugh. It was the first time he had ever seen how young she was when she laughed.

JOHN TAINTOR FOOTE

Allegheny

Henderson's Thunder and Jake Lavan's White Rose met at sea. It was a secret meeting, as far as the police were concerned, but two hundred gentlemen of the sporting and underworld managed to be present. They withdrew quietly from the lights and babble of Manhattan, proceeded singly or in small groups through the dark and odorous warehouse district of the East River, and arrived at the steamer *Lucy Hammond*, made fast to Pier 19.

Each one who boarded the *Lucy Hammond* that night gave up the sum of ten dollars freely and without regret. For the comparatively small sum mentioned they were to have the privilege of observing whether or not the female bull-terrier was more deadly than the male. Henderson's Thunder had destroyed the pit dogs of Greater New York and suburbs like a devouring flame. Ten or more canine warriors of the Pittsburgh district had died hard in the iron jaws of White Rose.

At the stroke of ten the *Lucy Hammond* slipped from her pier, dropped silently down the river and drew safely

74

away from Manhattan Island and its minions of the law. Out to sea she stole, down the Jersey coast she crept, and presently Thunder and White Rose faced each other for a bristling instant upon her moon-bathed deck.

There were voices, suppressed voices, all about them. "Two hundred on the Rose."

"You're on."

"A hundred more you've made a bad bet."

"Nope. I got enough."

"I'll bet five hundred to a thousand the dog stops her in thirty minutes."

"I've got that, pal. This guy can hold it."

"Back, gents! Everybody back! A match between Henderson's Thunder, champion of New York, and Lavan's White Rose, of Pittsburgh, at forty-five pounds, give or take three pounds—the dog gives a pound and a quarter. Back, gents, if you please, well back from the pit. Ready, Thunder? Ready, Rose? *Let 'em go!*"

An hour and forty minutes later the referee crossed the pit to where Jake Lavan was crouching, white-lipped and silent. For ten minutes or more Jake had ceased to whisper as though in prayer, "Come on, you Rose, come on."

"She's through," said the referee. "Don't you want to save her?"

Jake closed and unclosed his hands, and gave a last despairing look at the feeble efforts of White Rose to free herself from the abiding brindle jaws which held and shook her. He rose suddenly to his full height and flung up his hand at Tom Henderson. "Come on—break his hold!" he said hoarsely. "We quit!"

So ended the first encounter between Thunder and White Rose. In addition to disproving Mr. Kipling's poem, it led to a second and more amicable meeting.

As Jake Lavan stepped from the pit with White Rose, white no longer, in his arms, Tom Henderson called after him:

"She's as game as they ever come. I'd like a pup from her and him. What do you say?"

Jake glanced down at the crimson head of White Rose, resting limp across his forearm, then at Thunder, still on his feet but swaying drunkenly.

"If she lives—you're on," he said.

The indomitable White Rose was pitted with Death that night, and won. She arrived at health and strength a month later, and the six greedy atoms which ultimately squirmed at her side were splotched with brindle on pinky white. Also, in an astonishingly short time a bone must not be thrown among them. Little and soft and helpless they seemed, but each had a set of sharp puppy teeth, with which, over a bone, they would do instant, joyous, and bloody execution. It was not the snarling scuffle of other breeds, undertaken and ended lightly; it was the quiet and deadly warfare of the fighting bull-terrier, which goes, barring interference, to the finish.

White Rose, of course, adored them. Her remaining eye lost something of its bold assurance when she realized that six feet of steel chain limited the protection she could assure her offspring. Whenever one of them waddled beyond this safety zone, she became, for the first time in her heroic life, a prey to anxious fears.

She was confirmed in her anxiety one morning, when the puppies decided to investigate an ancient alley cat that chose a sunny spot at the corner of the house in which to brood upon his wrongs. The puppies advanced toward the dour and forbidding feline in column formation, the boldest at their head. The leader halted at a respectful distance from the cat and ventured an unimpressive puppy bark. Its effect was negligible, and he decided to assume a more intimate attitude. Drawing closer, he invited the silent stranger to a romp by executing a number of clumsy advances and retreats.

The tip of a long gray tail, lying moveless in the sunshine, began to twitch. It attracted the puppy's attention. It was a fascinating thing—so long and still and furry, with just the end moving slightly. He felt a keen desire to pick it up and shake it with mock ferocity. Better not venture this at first, perhaps. Why not dab it lightly with his paw? The idea grew in his mind. It finally possessed him utterly and at last moved him to action. He drew closer to that fascinating tail. An instant later he was on his back, his round pink stomach exposed to two lightning claw strokes. When he regained his feet the cat was gone and his co-investigators had fled. He returned dazedly to his frenzied mother, who, from then on, would launch herself from the kennel like a bolt of destruction at the slightest sound or shadow.

This proved an effective method of securing the privacy she desired. Few visitors cared to remain in the vicinity of White Rose, silent, open-mouthed, lunging on the chain. It was a good, stout chain, to be sure, but chains have been known to break. The thought destroyed the morale of milk-men, icemen, children, dogs and cats, impartially. The neighborhood learned that just to the rear of the Lavan house was a small kingdom ruled over by a white fury, entirely devoted to maternity, which they would do well to avoid.

Sol Litchenstein, however, was not of the neighborhood. He was not of any neighborhood. His goings and comings were bounded by the number of miles per day he could whack out of the forlorn thing of hide and bones which pulled his junk-piled wagon. He knew nothing of the hair-raising terror that was to be found in the Lavans' back yard.

White Rose was dozing in the kennel one afternoon. She had waived the responsibilities of motherhood for the moment, and was allowing herself the luxury of a dream. She was dreaming of the pit. She had broken the hold of her opponent, had wrestled him off his feet, and was about to fasten herself enduringly at the base of his neck, when she was rudely awakened.

"Ra-a-gs! Ra-a-gs! Papeer, Ra-a-gs!"

White Rose was up and out with one convulsive leap, scattering puppies in all directions. Sol Litchenstein missed his doom by a scant inch. He lost only a greasy corduroy cap and one trousers leg. As he fled blindly toward the alley and his wagon, as white as the whitest of the rags which it contained, there was a small wail of agony from the kennel. It did not continue long. It came from the leader in the cat investigation, who still bore two red scratches along his plump mid-section, and such as he are silent under pain.

When Jake Lavan returned from the rolling mill that evening he found White Rose licking a woebegone puppy which floundered and sprawled when she nosed him to his feet. When his mother had flung herself at the intruding Sol the chain had looped about one of the puppy's legs and crushed it, so Jake discovered, beyond repair.

Jake, although he could watch a pit dog take its punishment in a fair fight, was tender as a woman where animals were concerned. The puppy must be destroyed—that was evident. Jake examined the damaged leg again and, holding the puppy under his coat to shield it from the winter wind, moved reluctantly toward the Allegheny River, two blocks away.

As he emerged from the alley which paralleled his domain, he encountered Mose Trimble shuffling disconsolately down Humboldt Street.

"Want to earn a dime smoke?" asked Jake abruptly, as it came to him that another might relieve him of his dreaded business with the Allegheny.

Mose ceased his shuffle and rolled a yellowish eyeball at his questioner.

"What way?"

"Take this pup to the river and drown him."

"Whuffor?"

"He's through," explained Jake. "Broke his leg somehow."

Now Mose had looked upon bad gin when it is white until the early morning hours of the night before. He had slept all day and was just emerging in search of a drink with which to quench slightly the raging fires within him. He extended a shaking hand.

"Slip him to me, man," he said.

Jake placed the puppy in a huge chocolate-colored palm, produced a thin dime, parted with it, and retraced his steps up the alley. Mose, with more purpose in his shuffle than heretofore, moved on down Humboldt Street toward the river.

It had been snowing intermittently that afternoon; small flakes were falling even now; they showed white for an instant on Mose's face and neck before turning to moisture on his glistening black skin. The snow disturbed him not at all. He was anticipating the gulp of liquid consolation which he would presently tilt into his burning soul. As his small burden stirred uneasily he tightened his fingers about its body.

"Ain' no use gettin' fidgety, dawg," he told the puppy. "Come on 'long wid Mose."

The puppy stirred again and began to shake. In addition to the pain of its broken leg it missed the soft straw of the kennel, the huddling bodies of its brothers and sisters, the soothing presence of White Rose. Its tremors increased until they distracted Mose.

"Whuffor you shake?" he inquired. "You ain' gonna shake long. That ol' river stop your shakin'. Allegheny git you soon, my frien'; no use to shake."

But the puppy continued to shiver, and presently it emitted a low cry of loneliness and despair.

"Wha's wrong wid you?" Mose demanded, lifting the puppy up for inspection. It was white except for a brindle splotch over one eye and a brindle saddle on its back. The tip of its muzzle and its nose were pink. Its eyes were the vague blue of the very young; but its head, as it moved it restlessly from side to side, expressed the qualities of its race. Unswerving tenacity, indomitable fortitude were stamped indelibly on that blocky little head. Here was purpose, determination, character. Mose, helpless drifter that he was, could see it. "Howdy, mistuh?" he said with a shade of uneasy respect. Still staring at the puppy, he arrived at the end of a small wharf and found dark water at his feet.

The Allegheny, inky black between its snow-covered banks, was broken here and there by floating cakes of ice. Mose shivered and felt cold for the first time that day. The fingers of his right hand were growing numb, he noticed, but his left hand, which held the puppy, was quite comfortable.

"Ain't you warm in the hand," said Mose; then added, after a pause, "Well, here we is." He looked at the river again. Lights were beginning to spring up on the farther shore. They sent yellow reflections along the surface, which wavered on the black water and glittered on the floating cakes of ice. They made the river seem more ominous, more forbidding if possible, than before.

Mose regarded the expanse of water and ice gloomily for a moment. He advanced to the edge of the wharf, stooped and dipped a finger in the river, clutching the puppy against the breast of his thin coat as he did so. Withdrawing the finger with some haste and a grunt of disapproval, he turned and climbed the bank.

"Too cold," he said.

II

Christmas was coming. It was to be a wonderful Christmas that year. As evidence of the fact the drawers of the desk in the consulting-room of Herbert Bruce, M.D., contained many things which were not essential to the practice of medicine. Also, down in the darkest corner of the cellar stood an infant fir tree. Its hope of pointing majestically to the stars for a century or more was gone. It was to have a shorter and more brilliant career. It would assume an effulgent splendor for a day in accepting the principal part of the first Christmas of Herbert Lansmere Bruce, Jr.

Strictly speaking, this would not be his first Christmas. It was, as a matter of fact, his second Christmas. But his hands had refused to close over a celluloid rattle the year before and a shiny silver mug had been completely ignored. Surely it was safe to assume that such a Christmas was no Christmas at all.

Arriving at the above conclusion, Herbert Bruce, M.D., looked at his watch and discovered that it was five minutes past office hours. He closed the consulting-room door, returned to the desk and opened a lower drawer. As a miser gloats over his gold he hung above the contents of the drawer, seeing in his mind's eye the treasures which each box or package contained.

That knobby looking thing in the blue paper was the fire engine with its iron-gray team. That flat box was the fish pond. You fished with magnets for hooks. Each fish having a metal mouth, it was astonishing with what avidity they took the bait. Ah, what a pleasant world it would be if livelier fishes rose as promptly to the lure! The long package was an engine and the cars it pulled triumphantly around a circular track. That bit of roadbed would be the scene of many a calamitous wreck, no doubt. Soldiers were in the big flat box, both prancing cavalry and plodding troops afoot.

What was in the oblong box of gray cardboard? Bruce tried to remember, failed, and took the box from the drawer. Removing the cover he discovered a white rabbit with pink glass eyes and long pink-lined ears. Now, where did that come from? He hadn't bought it. "One of Julia's things," he thought, as he remembered that she had shopped with him one morning.

He lifted the rabbit from the box and examined it. From its furry stomach a key protruded unobtrusively. This key he proceeded to wind.

The effect on the white rabbit was electrical. It kicked madly until he set it on the desk and released it, whereupon it hopped briskly across the blotting pad, banged into a paper weight and caromed against the ink well.

"Hey, look out!" yelled Bruce. His warning was unheeded. The white rabbit plunged its head into the ink well, and kicked frantically.

Bruce rescued the rabbit and held it at arm's length until its kicking became a faint twitching of the limbs and at last ceased altogether. Then he bore it to a wash basin and let a water faucet remove the signs of its unfortunate experience. He dried the rabbit's head and whiskers with absorbent cotton and was replacing it in its box when someone knocked at the side door of the consulting-room, which led directly to the street. Bruce put the box on the desk, went to the door and opened it.

Mose shuffled into the room. He removed his hat with one hand, the other hand he held within his half-opened coat.

"Evenin', Doctuh," said he.

"Good evening," said Bruce. "What's the matter, hurt your arm?"

"No, suh," said Mose, "nuthin' wrong wid me." He shuffled his feet and coughed uneasily.

"Well, what is it? What do you want?"

"Doctuh, please suh. Is you a animal doctuh?"

"You mean a veterinary. No, I'm not a veterinary."

"You don't nevah tend animals?"

"No; I never attend animals."

Mose blinked thoughtfully over this statement, moved toward the door, halted and turned. "I looked thoo the window when I'm passin'," he said significantly. "That's how I happen in."

The look of accusation which accompanied the words could not be ignored. "What are you trying to get at, anyway?" asked the now puzzled Bruce.

Mose advanced a firm step. "If you ain' tendin' a rabbit when I look thoo that window jus' now, what is you doin'?"

The light of understanding broke upon Bruce. The corners of his mouth twitched, but the earnestness of his questioner restrained him from unseemly hilarity.

"I see," he said gravely. "Well, here's your rabbit." He took the white rabbit from its box and held it out for inspection. "It's a toy for my little son—Christmas, you know."

Mose blinked at the rabbit for a moment. "Sure fooled me," he admitted finally. "Thought I seen him a-kickin' and a-squirmin' . . ."

"You did," said Bruce, and gave the key a half turn.

At the first convulsive movement of the rabbit, there shot from Mose's coat a round little, fierce little head, its pink mouth wide, its eyes flaming, its forehead wrinkled with rage. It was apparent that the son of Thunder and White Rose disapproved of rabbits and would do battle with this one.

"Good Lord!" said Bruce. "How old is he?"

"Can't rightly say. I ain' had him long," Mose confessed. "Look like he's mighty young. If you be so kin' and lay dat rabbit away, Doctuh, please."

Bruce put the rabbit on the desk. The puppy grew quieter. The white furry thing was undoubtedly another of those creatures which scratch one on the stomach and then disappear. He watched it with smoldering eyes, growling softly, while Mose, holding him cupped in his hands, explained.

"I've heard of Lavan's dogs," said Bruce when Mose had finished. "He wouldn't tell you to drown a puppy, if there was a chance for it."

"It's jus' his laig, tha's all. Jus' his hin' laig."

"But I'm not a veterinary, I've told you once. Why didn't you drown him, as you were told."

Mose looked down at the puppy, then raised his eyes and met Bruce's half-amused, half-impatient glance.

"He was so warm in the han'," he explained simply.

There was a moment's silence.

"I see," said Bruce at last. "Well, let's have a look at him."

"Thank you, Doctuh."

"H'mm, double fracture—poor little cuss. Just one thing to do for him."

"Yessuh," said Mose, brightening.

Bruce laid the puppy gently on the desk blotter, strode to a wall cabinet and returned with a small sponge and a glass-stoppered bottle filled with a colorless liquid.

"This is the best thing for him," he said.

"Yessuh." Mose's face was alight with the supreme confidence of his race in the medicine man. "Shall I rub it on the laig, Doctuh? Or give it internal."

"Neither. I'll hold it to his nose."

"Nose! What you got?"

"Chloroform," said Bruce briskly, saturating the sponge.

Mose's face fell from the heights of expectancy to the depths of gloom. "Ain' nuthin' you can do, Doctuh?"

"Not a thing. You see, he—" The sentence remained unfinished as Bruce turned toward the sound of a thudding clatter on the desk and stared dumfounded at what he saw.

The son of Thunder and White Rose had never for an instant taken his eyes from the furry thing that scratched and disappeared. Suddenly he had found himself on the desk facing the creature. One leg refusing to aid him, he had found it hard to cross that broad expanse of green blotter, very hard; but he had finally succeeded in doing so. He was now, with the silent intensity of his breed, shaking the life out of his enemy.

Bruce hastened to the rescue of the white rabbit for the

second time. It was saved with difficulty and the loss of a tuft of fur, to which two small jaws were steadfastly attached. When it was safe in the drawer once more, the eyes of Bruce and Mose met.

"He's hell on wheels, ain't he, Doctuh?"

Bruce nodded. There followed a silence, in which the white man and the black stared at a small puppy with a broken leg, ridding its mouth of a tuft of fur. In the eyes of both was the same shining look. Civilize him as you please, make his color what you like, man still will worship the born fighter.

Bruce spoke first. "I'll see what I can do with a splint and plaster of Paris."

Mose beamed, then sobered suddenly. "One thing mo', Doctuh. I jus' don't happen to be financial right now."

"Oh, that's all right," said Bruce.

Two hours later Mose was again facing the snow-laden winter wind. His thirst, forgotten while he was absorbed in the wonders of surgery, was now raging once more. He felt for the reassuring dime in his pocket, located it, and headed for One-Eyed Johnson's place, an emporium devoted to serving members of his own race with food and drink. He was still a block from its warmth and hospitality when there came a whimper of distress from beneath his coat.

"Less noise from you," said Mose. "Ain' the doctuh fix you up all nice and good?"

But the whimper grew.

"Say, lay off me, dawg," Mose advised.

A sudden alarming thought left him so limp that his shuffle became a drag. "My Gawd—he's hongry!"

Grumbling, threatening, cursing the ever-growing whimper in his ears, Mose reached the haven that he sought. In he shuffled. He gave one look of supreme longing toward the bar, then slouched to the lunch counter. "Gimme some hambu'ger steak and a nickel's wuth of milk," was his order.

The patrons of One-Eyed Johnson's place crowded about him a moment later and watched interestedly as the whimper changed to a violent lapping and gobbling.

"Whose dawg?"

"Mine."

"Whar you git him?"

"Neveh min'."

"What's dat on his laig?"

"Plastuh Paris—he jus' been tended by a doctuh."

"Huh—look like a good one. What's his name?"

Mose hesitated for an instant, then straightened up and swept the attentive circle with an important eye. "I calls him Allegheny," he said.

III

A year slipped by, as years do. It made no noticeable improvement in Mose or his fortunes. He was occupied with what he described as odd jobs, while looking for "regulah wuck with good people," and remained the same impecunious drifter as before.

The change in Allegheny, however, was startling. He grew into a forty-eight-pound, steel-muscled song of war, which ran, diminuendo, from a heavy chest and head to a neatly tapered tail.

That a slight swelling on his left hind leg did not trouble him was proved by the agility he displayed in treeing cats, or in romps and mock battles with playfully inclined dogs.

The latter amusement was frowned upon by Mose, after an interview with Jake Lavan, whom they met on the street one day.

"What'll you take for him," asked Jake, when he had been told how Allegheny had escaped a watery grave.

"He ain' for sale," said Mose promptly.

Jake's appraising eye lingered on Allegheny a moment longer. "I tell you what I'll do," he decided at last. "I'll train him and pit him, and see how good he is. It looks to me like it would take an awful dog to stop him. He might win some coin for us."

"When do I git him back?" Mose inquired.

"Oh, I dunno. If he's good we'll keep him workin'."

"Kin I have him when he ain' fightin'?"

"Why, sure, if you'll feed him right. What do you want with him?"

"Jus' comp'ny. Jus' to ramble aroun' wid me."

Jake gave way to ironical laughter. "Do you think you can pit him, and then let him sashey around town? Listen, nigger—that's a fightin' dog. He's by Thunder out of White Rose."

"Shuh," exclaimed Mose. "He don't bother nothin' 'cep' cats. He's a good-natured dawg."

"Oh, he is, eh!" said Jake grimly. "Well, I'll tell you what he'd do—after he learns what he's for—he'd kill every kioodle in Pittsburgh, as fast as he got to 'em."

"Huh," said Mose uneasily, as he visioned the unpleasant consequences which would follow the sudden taking off of white folks' dogs by Allegheny. "I'll keep my eye on that gen'leman."

"Well, lemme give him a whirl," urged Jake. "What do you say?"

"I don' say nuthin'," said Mose, getting abruptly under way. "Come on, dawg."

At the next street corner Allegheny was advised to sing small and watch his step. "If you git uppity," he was warned, "bad times goin' to ketch you by the short hairs." From then on he was heaped with reproaches if he so much as looked in the direction of a canine that assumed a belligerent attitude, and even polite exchanges with friendly strangers were discouraged. "Jus' ten' to your own business, and take no chances wid nobody," he was told. "Min' your p's and q's, an' some day you git a home."

The home referred to was the stately mansion of the "good people" of Mose's dreams, who would furnish ease and comfort to a handy man and a "splendid watch dawg," in exchange for a leisurely performance of light duties.

Good people, however, who desired to add a handy man and a watch dog to their establishment were rare. Mose was bitterly aware of this fact as he plodded homeward one evening, after four hours with a post-hole digger under a beating sun. As he passed a brick and stucco dwelling with a sweep of lawn in front, he halted suddenly. His listless eye had taken in some gold letters on a black name plate. "Herbert Bruce, M.D.," he read. He repeated the name aloud and addressed Allegheny. "Come here, dawg." Allegheny reluctantly gave up sniffing a telephone post and approached.

"Look at dat sign," said Mose. "Look at it good. Dat's de vehy doctuh dat fix your laig. He move on away from whar he was and I ain' neveh seen him since. Now, here he is. You come on in along wid me an 'spress your thanks."

Allegheny, impressed, followed Mose sedately up the walk to the door beside the black and gold name plate. A maid informed them that the doctor was in the back yard, but could be called.

"Thank you kindly," said Mose; "I'll jus' go roun' and speak to him."

When Allegheny realized that their business lay in the rear of the premises, his dignity fled. He had never forgotten a certain humiliating experience of puppyhood, and cats are found more frequently in back yards than anywhere else. He shot around the house like a brindle and white flash, his pads rasping crisply on the cement walk.

There was no cat in the back yard, he discovered. There were three people—a man, a woman, and a child. It was a boy child, with earnest blue eyes, pouting cherry lips, and tousled red-gold hair. He was digging a hole in a pile of sand with a very small shovel. The man and woman were standing with an arm about each other, watching.

Allegheny was interested at once. He knew something about digging holes himself. He promptly jumped the boards that confined the sand pile and confronted the child.

Several things happened in quick succession. The man sprang forward with a shout, the woman gasped and grew pale, the child stared round-eyed into Allegheny's wide red mouth for an instant, then—

"Oo-oo, doggie!" said he, and flung himself promiscuously on Allegheny's neck.

Allegheny decided to greet a brother hole-digger with proper cordiality. He turned his head and spread a wet tongue across the small face that had been pressed against his rolling jaw muscles.

" 'At's all right, Doctuh," called Mose. "He won' hurt him."

"I see he won't," said Bruce huskily. "It's all right, Julia. It's all right, my dear." He turned in suppressed fury on Mose. "Why do you let a dog like that run into people's yards? You frightened us—you frightened my wife. What do you mean by it?"

" 'Scuse me, Doctuh," said Mose abashed. "I was jus' bringin' him in to 'spress his thanks."

"To what?"

"I see your name as I wuz passin'. Don't you 'membah me? 'Membah how he shake the rabbit? 'Membah how you fix his laig?"

"Well, well!" said Bruce, his anger vanishing. "I wondered how that job turned out. And this is that puppy!"

"Dat's him. I take off de splint in fo' weeks, like you say, an' he's good as new."

"Well, well!" Bruce repeated, as he eyed the mighty Allegheny with a touch of professional pride. "Let's see, which leg was it?"

"The left, Doctuh. Got a little swellin' on it, dat's all."

Bruce bent over Allegheny and attempted to examine the leg. "Let go of the doggie, little son. Daddy wants to see him."

"Doggie mine," said Herbert Bruce, Junior, firmly, and tightened his arms about Allegheny's neck.

"No, no. Let Daddy see him. That's a good boy."

"Do away! Doggie mine."

"Let Daddy have him, do you hear me?"

"Doggie mine! Doggie mine! Doggie mi-i-ine!"

"Julia."

Mrs. Bruce moved quietly forward, and presently Allegheny was freed; but the son and heir of the house of Bruce was dancing up and down on his sand pile emitting sounds of utter woe.

"Bad Mudder—doggie mine."

"Baby! Baby dear! You mustn't! This isn't my great big boy. This isn't mother's man. Aren't you ashamed!"

"I want 'at doggie."

Allegheny saved the situation. He had kept his eye on the hole in the sand pile from the first. He now approached it, gave it a brief examination, and went to work with such enthusiasm that a cataract of sand shot from between his hind legs as his head and flying forepaws rapidly sank from view.

Herbert Bruce, Junior, grew suddenly quiet. His mouth closed as his eyes grew wide. So swift was his transition from rage to joy that huge tears were still rolling to the sand below via his cheeks and chin as he rewarded Allegheny's efforts with a shriek of appreciation.

"See a doggie! Oo, see a doggie!"

"Yes, darling, he's helping Junior. Isn't that nice of him?" And so the skies were cleared.

It developed a few moments later that the ordered content-
ment of the Bruce establishment was threatened by a dreaded
and inevitable general house-cleaning. Mose, having mentioned
the names of a multitude of housewives to whom he had
proved a solace upon like occasions, was engaged to appear
the following Monday morning and become a staff and com-
forter.

"I kin hep you out all nex' week, Miz Bruce," he confided.
"Afteh that, can't say. I'm lookin' foh a reguluh place wid
good people. Jus' how much wuck could a handy man do
'roun' here, Doctuh?"

"Oh, we haven't enough for all of a man's time, Mose. Some
grass to cut, furnace looked after—that's about all."

"You got a shoffuh?"

The average human being is reasonably healthy; there are
many young doctors in the world, and bills for their services
are paid last of all.

"No," said Bruce, with something like a sigh. "I drive myself."

"I wash and polish in ga'age three weeks once," suggested
Mose dreamily. "Well, I'll be gettin' on. I wuck on a B. & O.
diner one time, when I relieve a sick frien', Miz Bruce. Yessum, I'll be here at eight o'clock, Monday mawnin', yessum."

He was as good as his word and, being a new broom, swept
clean. But Allegheny, early in the day, committed an indis-
cretion. A heavy rug was hoisted to a clothes-line and smitten
thunderously despite its writhings. Convinced that the rug
was alive, Allegheny rushed to Mose's aid and fastened himself to a corner of the thick Bokhara. Mose promptly turned
the beater upon his assistant, who withdrew crestfallen and
assumed the role of interested spectator. Mose addressed him
through a cloud of dust.

"Wha's got into you?" he inquired. "If Miz Bruce ketch you
a-shakin' her dinin'-room rug, you'll hit trouble. Look like
you lef' your senses home to-day. I seen you walkin' stiff-

legged by dat loud-mouth coal-yard dog when we come pass. You betta look out, mistuh; if you start fightin', you know where you'll lan'? On de end of a chain, dat's what you will."

The coal-yard dog Mose referred to was Tiger, a huge striped and sullen Great Dane owned by the yard boss of the Pocahontas Coal Company.

It was Tiger's custom to lie in the doorway of the company's stables and indulge in watchful waiting. A dog might pass unchallenged if he kept steadfastly on his way, but if he lingered to investigate a tree or the fence, Tiger would gallop forth with a heart-shaking bellow that sent most loiterers flying down the street. Allegheny had not fled when he heard the foghorn voice of Tiger for the first time. He had waited motionless with raised head until the lumbering giant was upon him, looked him in the eye for an instant, exchanged sniffs with him, and trotted calmly on. Mose and he had passed the coal company's stables many times since then. Tiger's challenge and Allegheny's reception of it had always been the same. That morning there had been a change. At sight of Allegheny Tiger had appeared, as usual, but with this difference: he was growling, not barking, as he came. Then, as he drew near, Allegheny saw his eyes, and in those bloodshot eyes was an unknown something that Allegheny loathed and feared.

Ten feet away Tiger halted. He glared at Allegheny for a moment, then slouched past him to the horse trough at the curb. Plunging his muzzle deep in the water he lapped and gulped noisily, leaving streaks of slaver on the surface. Allegheny turned and left the spot, as though walking on eggs.

Mose had observed the formality of Allegheny's withdrawal. He now dwelt on the episode at such length that Allegheny, after scratching an ear thoughtfully for a time, yawned and laid down.

"You chase that wearisome look off your face," said Mose severely, "an' listen good. I carry some knickknacks up in the attic a while ago. You know what I fin' up there? Lot of ole fuhniture. Bed, washstan', chairs—jus' layin' there ketchin' dus', ain' doin' no good for itself or nobody. You know what's up oveh de ga'age? Nice big room, nothin' in it but a wuck-bench." Mose took the rug from the line, hoisted it to his shoulder, and started for the house. "You min' your p's and q's like I tell you," was his parting advice. "Can't neveh tell what's gonna happen."

Allegheny, left to his own devices, found them stale and unprofitable. He had resigned himself to complete boredom when a screened door banged and a small figure in blue rompers appeared with a pail and shovel.

"Oo-oo, doggie!"

Allegheny's pensive attitude vanished. There was a meeting which involved a passionate embrace and a wildly wagging tail. There were shrieks of rapture and deep barks of delight. There was a rush to the sand pile, where marvels of excavation were accomplished, under the command of a chief engineer who breathed hard and indicated with sandy fingers the spot where Allegheny was to dig "anozzer one."

The mother of the chief engineer was also fully occupied. Her problem was the removal of dirt, not its excavation; but she managed to glance out the window every moment or so at the scene of her son's endeavors.

Two busy hours fled by. Allegheny unearthed a piece of rubber hose half buried in the sand. It served as an excellent instrument for tug-of-war, and brought such shrieks of rapture from the chief engineer that his mother flew to a window. Her face cleared at what she saw.

"Careful, Junior!" she called. "Let go if he pulls too hard." She was turning from the window when she paused, listening.

From so far away that she had barely heard it had come a pistol shot. Others followed in rapid succession, until six shots were fired. She wondered vaguely what they meant, and again would have turned from the window, but now she heard, from somewhere down the street, faint shouts and screams, and as she listened they drew nearer.

Two painters were passing carrying buckets, brushes and a ladder. One of them looked back over his shoulder and did a curious thing. He dropped his bucket and brush, jerked the ladder from the other painter and set it against a tree. Then both painters climbed the ladder hastily just as a dog appeared, a huge dog, running in the middle of the street.

There was a horse hitched to a delivery wagon standing before the house next door. The dog sprang at the horse, snapping his great jaws. The horse reared, shook the dog off and ran away, with the wagon bouncing along behind him. A wheel of the wagon struck the dog and knocked him down. He got to his feet again and broke into a heavy, lurching run. The mother of the chief engineer screamed as only mothers scream, for the dog turned at the Bruces' drive and came into the yard.

Allegheny heard the scream. He dropped his end of the piece of rubber hose, looked inquiringly toward the house, and suddenly became a statue. . . . Tiger was lumbering up the drive, his mouth dripping slaver, his head swaying from side to side.

"Oo-oo," said the chief engineer. "Anozzer doggie."

But the hair on Allegheny's back lifted into a stiff ridge, for the eyes of Tiger, far worse than in the morning, were the eyes of a dog no longer; they belonged in a devil from hell.

"Nice doggie," cooed the chief engineer, with outstretched dimpled arms. The distance between those arms and Tiger lessened, lessened!—then something shot between. It was a forty-eight-pound fighting machine that was going into action at last. . . . Tiger went down, with Allegheny fastened to his throat.

The hair on Allegheny's back lifted into a stiff ridge.

There followed a battle which seemed one-sided. In noise and weight Allegheny was outclassed. He appeared to have no chance against the huge demented beast that roared like a lion as he struggled; but Jake Lavan, or Bill Henderson, or any of the gentlemen who had spent an interesting evening on the *Lucy Hammond* two years before, would not have wagered on the Great Dane had they been present. Having noticed that the bull-terrier had a throat hold, they would have bet their money on the silent-fighting son of Thunder and White Rose.

And Allegheny proved true to the blood that was in him, by holding on. He was flung against the fence, and held on. He was beaten like a flail on the cement walk, and held on. He was ground into the sand of the sand pile, and held on.

The weeping chief engineer was snatched to safety by his wild-eyed mother. Men gathered timidly in the street before the house. Mose came running, and Herbert Bruce, M.D., and at last a sweating policeman, while Allegheny held on.

The policeman had fired six shots at Tiger some little time before. He now fired a seventh from a two-inch range and did not miss. He might have saved his powder had he cared to. Tiger's roars had sunk to a choking rattle when the bullet entered his brain. For, under his great carcass, half buried in the sand, was Allegheny—still holding on.

"There's no danger," Bruce told the policeman a few moments later. "There isn't a tooth mark on him. He hasn't the smallest scratch. Here, look for yourself."

"He's been fightin' wid a mad dog," insisted the policeman, flourishing his gun.

Bruce caught the weapon in his hand and forced the muzzle to the ground. "Put it up, Tim," he urged. "I'll send him to a veterinary hospital for thirty days. If he doesn't show hydrophobia in that time, he never will."

But the policeman shook his head. "Let go the gun, sohrr. I'm sorry, but it's got to be done."

Then Herbert Bruce, M.D., played his trump card. Having brought a small Irishman into the world the summer before, he now looked the proud father steadily in the eye.

"Tim," said he, "he saved my boy. He saved my little son—"

The policeman shifted his glance. He took in the panting Allegheny, caught the pleading eyes of Mose, and looked down at the revolver in his hand.

"If ye could git a permit from the boord av health—" he began. And so a second battle was won.

As a result of it, Allegheny was taken to the hospital that afternoon, but seemed likely to return, for Mose spent the evening moving furniture from the attic to the room over the garage, and when the chief engineer wailed for his "doggie" at bedtime his mother took him in her arms and held him very close.

"He's gone away for just a little while," said she. "When he comes back, you'll have him every day."

SAMUEL A. DERIEUX

The Comet

No PUPPY ever came into the world under more favorable conditions than Comet. He was descended from a famous family of pointers. Both his mother and father were champions. Before he opened his eyes, while he was still crawling about over his brothers and sisters, blind as puppies are at birth, Jim Thompson, Mr. Devant's kennel master, picked him out:

"That's the best un in the bunch."

When he was only three weeks old, he pointed a butterfly that lit in the yard in front of his nose.

"Come here, Molly," yelled Jim to his wife. "Pointed—the little cuss!"

When Thompson started taking the growing pups out of the yard, into the fields to the side of the Devants' great Southern winter home, Oak Knob, it was Comet who strayed farthest from the man's protecting care. And when Jim taught them all to follow when he said "Heel," to drop when he said "Drop," and to stand stock-still when he said "Ho," he learned far more quickly than the others.

At six months he set his first covey of quail, and remained perfectly staunch. "He's goin' to make a great dog," said Thompson. Everything—size, muscle, nose, intelligence, earnestness, pointed to the same conclusion. Comet was one of the favored of the gods.

One day, after the leaves had turned red and brown and the mornings grown chilly, a crowd of people, strangers to him, arrived at Oak Knob. Then out of the house with Thompson came a big man in tweed clothes, and the two walked straight to the curious young dogs, who were watching them with shining eyes and wagging tails.

"Well, Thompson," said the big man. "Which is the future champion you've been writing me about?"

"Pick him out for yourself, sir," said Thompson confidently.

After that they talked a long time planning for the future of Comet. His yard training was now over (Thompson was only yard trainer), and he must be sent to a man experienced in training and handling for field trials.

"Larsen's the man to bring him out," said the big man in tweeds, who was George Devant himself. "I saw his dogs work in the Canadian Derby."

Thompson spoke hesitatingly, apologetically, as if he hated to bring the matter up. "Mr. Devant, . . . you remember, sir, a long time ago Larsen sued us for old Ben."

"Yes, Thompson; I remember, now that you speak of it."

"Well, you remember the court decided against him, which was the only thing it could do, for Larsen didn't have any more right to that dog than the Sultan of Turkey. But, Mr. Devant, I was there, and I saw Larsen's face when the case went against him."

Devant looked keenly at Thompson.

"Another thing, Mr. Devant," Thompson went on, still

hesitatingly; "Larsen had a chance to get hold of this breed of pointers and lost out, because he dickered too long, and acted cheesy. Now they've turned out to be famous. Some men never forget a thing like that. Larsen's been talkin' these pointers down ever since, sir."

"Go on," said Devant.

"I know Larsen's a good trainer. But it'll mean a long trip for the young dog to where he lives. Now, there's an old trainer lives near here, Wade Swygert. There never was a straighter man than him. He used to train dogs in England."

Devant smiled. "Thompson, I admire your loyalty to your friends; but I don't think much of your business sense. We'll turn over some of the others to Swygert, if he wants 'em. Comet must have the best. I'll write Larsen tonight, Thompson. Tomorrow, crate Comet and send him off."

Just as no dog ever came into the world under more favorable auspices, so no dog ever had a bigger "send off" than Comet. Even the ladies of the house came out to exclaim over him, and Marian Devant, pretty, eighteen, and a sportswoman, stooped down, caught his head between her hands, looked into his fine eyes and wished him "Good luck, old man." In the living-room the men laughingly drank toasts to his future, and from the high-columned portico Marian Devant waved him good-by, as in his clean padded crate, he was driven off, a bewildered youngster, to the station.

Two days and two nights he traveled, and at noon of the third day, at a lonely railroad station in a prairie country that rolled like a heavy sea, he was lifted, crate and all, off the train. A lean, pale-eyed, sanctimonious-looking man came toward him.

"Some beauty that, Mr. Larsen," said the agent as he helped Larsen's man lift the crate onto a small truck.

"Yes," drawled Larsen in a meditative voice, "pretty enough to look at—but he looks scared—er—timid."

"Of course he's scared," said the agent; "so would you be if they was to put you in some kind of a whale of a balloon an' ship you in a crate to Mars."

The station agent poked his hands through the slats and patted the head. Comet was grateful for that, because everything was strange. He had not whined nor complained on the trip, but his heart had pounded fast, and he had been homesick.

And everything continued to be strange: the treeless country through which he was driven, the bald house, and huge barns where he was lifted out, the dogs that crowded about him when he was turned into the kennel yard. These eyed him with enmity and walked round and round him. But he stood his ground staunchly for a youngster, returning fierce look for fierce look, growl for growl, until the man called him away and chained him to a kennel.

For days Comet remained chained, a stranger in a strange land. Each time at the click of the gate announcing Larsen's entrance, he sprang to his feet from force of habit, and stared hungrily at the man for the light he was accustomed to see in human eyes. But with just a glance at him, the man would turn one or more of the other dogs loose and ride off to train them.

But he was not without friends of his own kind. Now and then another young dog (he alone was chained up) would stroll his way with wagging tail, or lie down near by, in that strange bond of sympathy that is not confined to man. Then Comet would feel better and would want to play, for he was still half puppy. Sometimes he would pick up a stick and shake it, and his partner would catch the other end. They would tug and growl with mock ferocity, and then lie down and look at each other curiously.

If any attention had been paid him by Larsen, Comet would

have quickly overcome his feeling of strangeness. He was no milksop. He was like an overgrown boy, off at college, or in some foreign city. He was sensitive, and not sure of himself. Had Larsen gained his confidence, it would all have been different. And as for Larsen—he knew that perfectly well.

One fine sunny afternoon, Larsen entered the yard, came straight to him, and turned him loose. In the exuberance of his spirits he ran round and round the yard, barking in the faces of his friends. Larsen let him out, mounted a horse and commanded him to heel. He obeyed with wagging tail.

A mile or more down the road, Larsen turned off into the fields. Across his saddle was something the young pointer had had no experience with—a gun. That part of his education Thompson had neglected, at least put off, for he had not expected that Comet would be sent away so soon. That was where Thompson had made a mistake.

At the command "Hi on" the young pointer ran eagerly around the horse, and looked up into the man's face to be sure he had heard aright. At something he saw there, the tail and ears drooped momentarily, and there came over him again a feeling of strangeness, almost of dismay. Larsen's eyes were mere slits of blue glass, and his mouth was set in a thin line.

At a second command, though, he galloped off swiftly, boldly. Round and round an extensive field of straw he circled, forgetting any feeling of strangeness now, every fiber of his being intent on the hunt, while Larsen, sitting on his horse, watched him with appraising eyes.

Suddenly there came to Comet's nose the smell of game birds, strong, pungent, compelling. He stiffened into an earnest, beautiful point. Heretofore in the little training he had had, Thompson had come up behind him, flushed the birds, and made him drop. And now Larson, having quickly dismounted and tied his horse, came up behind him, just as Thompson had done, except that in Larsen's hand was the gun.

The old-fashioned black powder of a generation ago makes a loud explosion. It sounds like a cannon, compared with the modern smokeless powder, now used by all hunters. Perhaps it was only an accident that had caused Larsen before he left the house to load his pump gun with black powder shells.

As for Comet he only knew that the birds rose; then above his head burst an awful roar, almost splitting his tender ear drums, shocking every sensitive nerve, filling him with terror such as he had never felt before. Even then, in the confusion and horror of the surprise, he turned to the man, head ringing, eyes dilated. A single reassuring word, and he would have steadied. As for Larsen, though, he declared afterward (to others and to himself even) that he noticed no nervousness in the dog; that he was only intent on getting several birds for breakfast.

Twice, three times, four times, the pump gun bellowed in its cannon-like roar, piercing the ear drums, shattering the nerves. Comet turned; one more glance backward at a face, strange, exultant—and then the puppy in him conquered. Tail tucked, he ran away from that shattering noise.

Miles he ran. Now and then, stumbling over briars, he yelped. Not once did he look back. His tail was tucked, his eyes crazy with fear. Seeing a house, he made for that. It was the noon hour and a group of farm hands was gathered in the yard. One of them, with a cry "Mad dog," ran into the house after a gun. When he came out, they told him the dog was under the porch. And so he was. Pressed against the wall, in the darkness, the magnificent young pointer with the quivering soul waited, panting, eyes gleaming, the horror still ringing in his ears.

Here Larsen found him that afternoon. A boy crawled underneath the porch and dragged him out. He, who had started life favored of the gods, who that morning even had been full of high spirits, who had circled a field like a champion, was now a cringing, shaking creature, like a homeless cur.

And thus it happened that Comet came home, in disgrace— a gun-shy dog, a coward, expelled from college, not for some youthful prank, but because he was—yellow. And he knew he was disgraced. He saw it in the face of the big man, Devant, who looked at him in the yard where he had spent his happy puppyhood, then turned away. He knew it because of what he saw in the face of Jim Thompson.

In the house was a long and plausible letter, explaining how it had happened:

> I did everything I could. I never was as surprised in my life. The dog's hopeless.

As for the other inhabitants of the big house, their minds were full of the events of the season: de luxe hunting parties, more society events than hunts; lunches in the woods served by uniformed butlers; launch rides up the river; arriving and departing guests. Only one of them, except Devant himself, gave the gun-shy dog a thought. Marian Devant came out to visit him in his disgrace. She stooped before him as she had done on that other and happier day, and again caught his head between her hands. But his eyes did not meet hers, for in his dim way he knew he was not now what he had been.

"I don't believe he's yellow—inside!" she declared, looking up at Thompson, her cheeks flushed.

Thompson shook his head.

"I tried him with a gun, Miss Marian," he declared. "I just showed it to him, and he ran into his kennel."

"I'll go get mine. He won't run from me."

But at sight of her small gun it all came back. Again he

seemed to hear the explosion that had shattered his nerves. The terror had entered his very soul. In spite of her pleading, he made for his kennel. Even the girl turned away from him now. And as he lay panting in the shelter of his kennel he knew that never again would men look at him as they had looked, or life be sweet to him as it had been.

Then there came to Oak Knob an old man, to see Thompson. He had been on many seas, he had fought in a dozen wars, and had settled at last on a little truck farm near by. Somewhere, in his life full of adventure and odd jobs, he had trained dogs and horses. His face was lined and seamed, his hair was white, his eyes piercing, blue and kind. Wade Swygert was his name.

"There's been dirty work," he said, when he looked at the dog. "I'll take him if you're goin' to give him away."

Give him away—who had been Championship hope!

Marian Devant came out and looked into the face of the old man, shrewdly, understandingly.

"Can you cure him?" she demanded.

"I doubt it, miss," was the sturdy answer.

"You will try?"

The blue eyes lighted up. "Yes, I'll try."

"Then you can have him. And—if there's any expense—"

"Come, Comet," said the old man.

That night, in a neat, humble house, Comet ate supper placed before him by a stout old woman, who had followed this old man to the ends of the world. That night he slept before their fire. Next day he followed the old man all about the place. Several days and nights passed this way, then, while he lay before the fire, old Swygert came in with a gun. At sight of it, Comet sprang to his feet. He tried to rush out of the room, but the doors were closed. Finally, he crawled under the bed.

Every night after that Swygert got out the gun, until he

crawled under the bed no more. Finally, one day the man fastened the dog to a tree in the yard, then came out with a gun. A sparrow lit in a tree, and he shot it. Comet tried to break the rope. All his panic had returned; but the report had not shattered him as that other did, for the gun was loaded light.

After that, frequently the old man shot a bird in his sight, loading the gun more and more heavily, and each time after the shot, coming to him, showing him the bird, and speaking to him kindly, gently. But for all that the terror remained in his heart.

One afternoon the girl, accompanied by a young man, rode over on horseback, dismounted and came in. She always stopped when she was riding by.

"It's mighty slow business," old Swygert reported; "I don't know whether I'm makin' any headway or not."

That night old Mrs. Swygert told him she thought he had better give it up. It wasn't worth the time and worry. The dog was just yellow.

Swygert pondered a long time. "When I was a kid," he said at last, "there came up a terrible thunderstorm. It was in South America. I was water boy for a railroad gang, and the storm drove us in a shack. While lightnin' was hittin' all around, one of the grown men told me it always picked out boys with red hair. My hair was red, an' I was little and ignorant. For years I was skeered of lightnin'. I never have quite got over it. But no man ever said I was yellow."

Again he was silent for a while. Then he went on: "I don't seem to be makin' much headway, I admit that. I'm lettin' him run away as far as he can. Now I've got to shoot an' make him come toward the gun himself, right while I'm shootin' it."

Next day Comet was tied up and fasted, and next, until he was gaunt and famished. Then, on the afternoon of the third day, Mrs. Swygert, at her husband's direction, placed before him, within reach of his chain, some raw beefsteak. As he started for it, Swygert shot. He drew back, panting, then, hunger getting the better of him, started again. Again Swygert shot.

After that for days Comet "Ate to music," as Swygert expressed it. "Now," he said, "he's got to come toward the gun when he's not even tied up."

Not far from Swygert's house is a small pond, and on one side the banks are perpendicular. Toward this pond the old man, with the gun under his arm and the dog following, went. Here in the silence of the woods, with just the two of them together, was to be a final test.

On the shelving bank Swygert picked up a stick and tossed it into the middle of the pond with the command to "fetch." Comet sprang eagerly in and retrieved it. Twice this was repeated. But the third time, as the dog approached the shore, Swygert picked up the gun and fired.

Quickly the dog dropped the stick, then turned and swam toward the other shore. Here, so precipitous were the banks, he could not get a foothold. He turned once more and struck out diagonally across the pond. Swygert met him and fired.

Over and over it happened. Each time, after he fired, the old man stooped down with extended hand and begged him to come on. His face was grim now, and though the day was cool sweat stood out on his brow. "You'll face the music," he said, "or you'll drown. Better be dead than called yellow."

The dog was growing weary now. His head was barely above water. His efforts to clamber up the opposite bank were feeble, frantic. Yet, each time as he drew near the shore Swygert fired.

He was not using light loads now. He was using the regular load of the bird hunter. Time had passed for temporizing. The sweat was standing out all over his face. The sternness in his eyes was terrible to see, for it was the sternness of a man who is suffering.

A dog can swim a long time. The sun dropped over the trees. Still the firing went on, regularly, like a minute gun.

Just before the sun set an exhausted dog staggered toward an old man, almost as exhausted as he. The dog had been too near death and was too faint to care now for the gun that was being fired over his head. On and on he came, toward the man, disregarding the noise of the gun. It would not hurt him, that he knew at last. He might have many enemies, but the gun, in the hands of this man, was not one of them. Suddenly old Swygert sank down and took the dripping dog in his arms.

"Old boy," he said, "old boy."

That night Comet lay before the fire, and looked straight into the eyes of a man, as he used to look in the old days.

Next season, Larsen, glancing over his sporting papers, was astonished to see that among promising Derbys the fall trials had called forth was a pointer named Comet. He would have thought it some other dog than the one who had disappointed him so by turning out gun-shy, in spite of all his efforts to prevent, had it not been for the fact that the entry was booked as Comet; owner, Miss Marian Devant; handler, Wade Swygert.

Next year he was still more astonished to see in the same paper that Comet, handled by Swygert, had won first place in a Western trial, and was prominently spoken of as a National Championship possibility. As for him, he had no young entries to offer, but was staking everything on the National Championship, where he was to enter Larsen's Peerless II.

It was strange how things fell out—but things have a habit of turning out strangely in field trials, as well as elsewhere. When Larsen reached the town where the National Championship was to be run, there on the street, straining at the leash held by old Swygert, whom he used to know, was a seasoned young pointer, with a white body, a brown head and a brown saddle spot—the same pointer he had seen two years before turn tail and run in that terror a dog never quite overcomes.

But the strangest thing of all happened that night at the drawing, when, according to the slips taken at random from a hat, it was declared that on the following Wednesday, Comet, the pointer, was to run with Peerless II.

It gave Larsen a strange thrill, this announcement. He left the meeting and went straightway to his room. There for a long time he sat pondering. Next day at a hardware store he bought some black powder, and some shells.

The race was to be run next day, and that night in his room he loaded half a dozen shells. It would have been a study in faces to watch him as he bent over his work, on his lips a smile. Into the shells he packed all the powder they could stand, all the powder his trusted gun could stand, without bursting. It was a load big enough to kill a bear, to bring down a buffalo. It was a load that would echo and reëcho in the hills.

On the morning that Larsen walked out in front of the judges and the field, Peerless II at the leash, Old Swygert with Comet at his side, he glanced around at the "field," or spectators. Among them was a handsome young woman, and with her, to his amazement, George Devant. He could not help chuckling inside himself as he thought of what would happen that day, for once a gun-shy dog, always a gun-shy dog—that was *his* experience.

As for Comet, he faced the straw fields eagerly, confidently, already a veteran. Long ago fear of the gun had left him, for the most part. There were times, when at a report above his head, he still trembled, and the shocked nerves in his ear gave a twinge like that of a bad tooth. But always at the quiet voice of the old man, his god, he grew steady, and remained staunch.

Some disturbing memory did start within him today as he glanced at the man with the other dog. It seemed to him as if in another and an evil world he had seen that face. His heart began to pound fast, and his tail drooped for a moment. Within an hour it was all to come back to him—the terror, the panic, the agony of that far-away time.

He looked up at old Swygert, who was his god, and to whom his soul belonged, though he was booked as the property of Miss Marian Devant. Of the arrangements he could know nothing, being a dog. Old Swygert, having cured him, could not meet the expenses of taking him to field trials. The girl had come to the old man's assistance, an assistance which he had accepted only under condition that the dog should be entered as hers, with himself as handler.

"Are you ready, gentlemen?" the judges asked.

"Ready," said Larsen and old Swygert.

And Comet and Peerless II were speeding away across that field, and behind them came handlers, and judges and spectators, all mounted.

It was a race people still talk about, and for a reason, for strange things happened that day. At first there was nothing unusual. It was like any other field trial. Comet found birds, and Swygert, his handler, flushed them and shot. Comet remained steady. Then Peerless II found a covey, and Larsen flushed them and shot. And so for an hour it went.

Then Comet disappeared, and old Swygert, riding hard and looking for him, went out of sight over a hill. But Comet had not gone far. As a matter of fact he was near by, hidden in some high straw, pointing a covey of birds. One of the spectators spied him, and called the judges' attention to him. Everybody, including Larsen, rode up to him, but still Swygert had not come back.

They called him, but the old man was a little deaf. Some of the men rode to the top of the hill, but could not see him. In his zeal, he had got a considerable distance away. Meanwhile, here was his dog, pointed.

If anyone had looked at Larsen's face he would have seen the exultation there, for now his chance had come—the very chance he had been looking for. It's a courtesy one handler sometimes extends another who is absent from the spot, to go in and flush his dog's birds.

"I'll handle this covey for Mr. Swygert," said Larsen to the judges, his voice smooth and plausible, on his face a smile.

And thus it happened that Comet faced his supreme ordeal without the steadying voice of his god.

He only knew that ahead of him were birds, and that behind him a man was coming through the straw, and that behind the man a crowd of people on horseback were watching him. He had become used to that, but when, out of the corner of his eye, he saw the face of the advancing man, his soul began to tremble.

"Call your dog in, Mr. Larsen," directed the judge. "Make him backstand."

Only a moment was lost, while Peerless, a young dog himself, came running in and at a command from Larsen stopped in his tracks behind Comet, and pointed. Larsen's dogs always obeyed, quickly, mechanically. Without ever gaining their confidence, Larsen had a way of turning them into finished field-trial dogs. They obeyed, because they were afraid not to.

According to the rules the man handling the dog has to shoot as the birds rise. This is done in order to test the dog's steadiness when a gun is fired over him. No specification is made as to the size of the shotgun to be used. Usually, however, small-gauge guns are carried. The one in Larsen's hands was a twelve gauge, and consequently large.

All morning he had been using it over his own dog. Nobody had paid any attention to it, because he shot smokeless powder. But now, as he advanced, he reached into the left-hand pocket of his hunting coat, where six shells rattled as he hurried along. Two of these he took out and rammed into the barrels.

As for Comet, still standing rigid, statuesque, he heard, as has been said, the brush of steps through the straw, glimpsed a face, and trembled. But only for a moment. Then he steadied, head high, tail straight out. The birds rose with a whirr—and then was repeated that horror of his youth. Above his ears, ears that would always be tender, broke a great roar. Either because of his excitement, or because of a sudden wave of revenge, or of a determination to make sure of the dog's flight, Larsen had pulled both triggers at once. The combined report shattered through the dog's ear drums, it shivered through his nerves, he sank in agony into the straw.

Then the old impulse to flee was upon him, and he sprang to his feet, and looked about wildly. But from somewhere in that crowd behind him came to his tingling ears a voice—clear, ringing, deep, the voice of a woman—a woman he knew —pleading as his master used to plead, calling on him not to run, but to stand.

"Steady," it said. "Steady, Comet!"

It called him to himself, it soothed him, it calmed him, and he turned and looked toward the crowd. With the roar of the shotgun the usual order observed in field trials was broken up. All rules seemed to have been suspended. Ordinarily no one belonging to "the field" is allowed to speak to a dog. Yet the girl had spoken to him. Ordinarily, the spectators must remain in the rear of the judges. Yet one of the judges had himself wheeled his horse about and was galloping off, and Marian Devant had pushed through the crowd and was riding toward the bewildered dog.

He stood staunch where he was, though in his ears was still a throbbing pain, and though all about him was this growing confusion he could not understand. The man he feared was running across the field yonder, in the direction taken by the judge. He was blowing his whistle as he ran. Through the crowd, his face terrible to see, his own master was coming. Both the old man and the girl had dismounted now, and were running toward him.

"I heard," old Swygert was saying to her. "I heard it! I might 'a' known! I might 'a' known!"

"He stood," she panted, "like a rock—oh, the brave, beautiful thing!"

"Where is that—" Swygert suddenly checked himself and looked around.

A man in the crowd (they had all gathered about now), laughed.

"He's gone after his dog," he said. "Peerless has run away!"

ERIC KNIGHT

Lassie Come-Home

The dog had met the boy by the school gate for five years. Now she couldn't understand that times were changed and she wasn't supposed to be there any more. But the boy knew.

So when he opened the door of the cottage, he spoke before he entered.

"Mother," he said, "Lassie's come home again."

He waited a moment, as if in hope of something. But the man and woman inside the cottage did not speak.

"Come in, Lassie," the boy said.

He held open the door, and the tricolor collie walked in obediently. Going head down, as a collie when it knows something is wrong, it went to the rug and lay down before the hearth, a black-white-and-gold aristocrat. The man, sitting on a low stool by the fireside, kept his eyes turned away. The woman went to the sink and busied herself there.

"She were waiting at school for me, just like always," the boy went on. He spoke fast, as if racing against time. "She must ha' got away again. I thought, happen this time, we might just——"

"No!" the woman exploded.

The boy's carelessness dropped. His voice rose in pleading.

"But this time, mother! Just this time. We could hide her. They wouldn't ever know."

"Dogs, dogs, dogs!" the woman cried. The words poured from her as if the boy's pleading had been a signal gun for her own anger. "I'm sick o' hearing about tykes round this house. Well, she's sold and gone and done with, so the quicker she's taken back the better. Now get her back quick, or first thing ye know we'll have Hynes round here again. Mr. Hynes!"

Her voice sharpened in imitation of the Cockney accent of the south: "Hi know you Yorkshiremen and yer come-'ome dogs. Training yer dogs to come 'ome so's yer can sell 'em hover and hover again.

"Well, she's sold, so ye can take her out o' my house and home to them as bought her!"

The boy's bottom lip crept out stubbornly, and there was silence in the cottage. Then the dog lifted its head and nudged the man's hand, as a dog will when asking for patting. But the man drew away and stared, silently, into the fire.

The boy tried again, with the ceaseless guile of a child, his voice coaxing.

"Look, feyther, she wants thee to bid her welcome. Aye, she's that glad to be home. Happen they don't tak' good care on her up there? Look, her coat's a bit poorly, don't ye think? A bit o' linseed strained through her drinking water—that's what I'd gi' her."

Still looking in the fire, the man nodded. But the woman, as if perceiving the boy's new attack, sniffed.

"Aye, tha wouldn't be a Carraclough if tha didn't know more about tykes nor breaking eggs wi' a stick. Nor a York-shireman. My goodness, it seems to me sometimes that chaps in this village thinks more on their tykes nor they do o' their own flesh and blood. They'll sit by their firesides and let their own bairns starve so long as t' dog gets fed."

The man stirred, suddenly, but the boy cut in quickly.

"But she does look thin. Look, truly—they're not feeding her right. Just look!"

"Aye," the woman chattered. "I wouldn't put it past Hynes to steal t' best part o' t' dog meat for himself. And Lassie always was a strong eater."

"She's fair thin now," the boy said.

Almost unwillingly the man and woman looked at the dog for the first time.

"My gum, she is off a bit," the woman said. Then she caught herself. "Ma goodness, I suppose I'll have to fix her a bit o' summat. She can do wi' it. But soon as she's fed, back she goes. And never another dog I'll have in my house. Never another. Cooking and nursing for 'em, and as much trouble to bring up as a bairn!"

So, grumbling and chatting as a village woman will, she moved about, warming a pan of food for the dog. The man and boy watched the collie eat. When it was done, the boy took from the mantelpiece a folded cloth and a brush, and began prettying the collie's coat. The man watched for several minutes, and then could stand it no longer.

"Here," he said.

He took the cloth and brush from the boy and began working expertly on the dog, rubbing the rich, deep coat, then brushing the snowy whiteness of the full ruff and the apron, bringing out the heavy leggings on the forelegs. He lost himself in his work, and the boy sat on the rug, watching contentedly. The woman stood it as long as she could.

"Now will ye please tak' that tyke out o' here?"

The man flared in anger.

"Well, ye wouldn't have me tak' her back looking like a mucky Monday wash, wouldta?"

He bent again, and began fluffing out the collie's petticoats.

"Joe!" the woman pleaded. "Will ye tak' her out o' here? Hynes'll be nosing round afore ye know it. And I won't have that man in my house. Wearing his hat inside, and going on like he's the duke himself—him and his leggings!"

"All right, lass."

"And this time, Joe, tak' young Joe wi' ye."

"What for?"

"Well, let's get the business done and over with. It's him that Lassie runs away for. She comes for young Joe. So if he went wi' thee, and told her to stay, happen she'd be content and not run away no more, and then we'd have a little peace and quiet in the home—though heaven knows there's not much hope o' that these days, things being like they are." The woman's voice trailed away, as if she would soon cry in weariness.

The man rose. "Come, Joe," he said. "Get thy cap."

The Duke of Rudling walked along the gravel paths of his place with his granddaughter, Philippa. Philippa was a bright and knowing young woman, allegedly the only member of the duke's family he could address in unspotted language. For it was also alleged that the duke was the most irascible, vile-tempered old man in the three Ridings of Yorkshire.

"Country going to pot!" the duke roared, stabbing at the walk with his great blackthorn stick. "When I was a young man! Hah! Women today not as pretty. Horses today not as fast. As for dogs—ye don't see dogs today like——"

Just then the duke and Philippa came round a clump of rhododendrons and saw a man, a boy and a dog.

"Ah," said the duke, in admiration. Then his brow knotted. "Damme, Carraclough! What're ye doing with my dog?"

He shouted it quite as if the others were in the next county, for it was also the opinion of the Duke of Rudling that people were not nearly so keen of hearing as they used to be when he was a young man.

"It's Lassie," Carraclough said. "She runned away again and I brought her back."

Carraclough lifted his cap, and poked the boy to do the same, not in any servile gesture, but to show that they were as well brought up as the next.

"Damme, ran away again!" the duke roared. "And I told that utter nincompoop Hynes to—where is he? Hynes! Hynes! Damme, Hynes, what're ye hiding for?"

"Coming, your lordship!" sounded a voice, far away behind the shrubberies. And soon Hynes appeared, a sharp-faced man in check coat, riding breeches, and the cloth leggings that grooms wear.

"Take this dog," roared the duke, "and pen her up! And damme, if she breaks out again, I'll—I'll——"

The duke waved his great stick threateningly, and then, without so much as a thank you or kiss the back of my hand to Joe Carraclough, he went stamping and muttering away.

"I'll pen 'er up," Hynes muttered, when the duke was gone. "And if she ever gets awye agyne, I'll——"

He made as if to grab the dog, but Joe Carraclough's hob-nailed boot trod heavily on Hynes' foot.

"I brought my lad wi' me to bid her stay, so we'll pen her up this time. Eigh—sorry! I didn't see I were on thy foot. Come, Joe, lad."

They walked down the crunching gravel path, along by the neat kennel buildings. When Lassie was behind the closed door, she raced into the high wire run where she could see them as they went. She pressed close against the wire, waiting.

The boy stood close, too, his fingers through the meshes touching the dog's nose.

"Go on, lad," his father ordered. "Bid her stay!"

The boy looked around, as if for help that he did not find. He swallowed, and then spoke, low and quickly.

"Stay here, Lassie, and don't come home no more," he said. "And don't come to school for me no more. Because I don't want to see ye no more. 'Cause tha's a bad dog, and we don't love thee no more, and we don't want thee. So stay there forever and leave us be, and don't never come home no more."

Then he turned, and because it was hard to see the path plainly, he stumbled. But his father, who was holding his head very high as they walked away from Hynes, shook him savagely, and snapped roughly: "Look where tha's going!"

Then the boy trotted beside his father. He was thinking that he'd never be able to understand why grownups sometimes were so bad-tempered with you, just when you needed them most.

After that, there were days and days that passed, and the dog did not come to the school gate any more. So then it was not like old times. There were so many things that were not like old times.

The boy was thinking that as he came wearily up the path and opened the cottage door and heard his father's voice, tense with anger: ". . . walk my feet off. If tha thinks I like——"

Then they heard his opening of the door and the voice stopped and the cottage was silent.

That's how it was now, the boy thought. They stopped talking in front of you. And this, somehow, was too much for him to bear.

He closed the door, ran out into the night, and onto the moor, that great flat expanse of land where all the people of that village walked in lonesomeness when life and its troubles seemed past bearing.

A long while later, his father's voice cut through the darkness.

"What's tha doing out here, Joe lad?"

"Walking."

"Aye."

They went on together, aimlessly, each following his own thoughts. And they both thought about the dog that had been sold.

"Tha maun't think we're hard on thee, Joe," the man said at last. "It's just that a chap's got to be honest. There's that to it. Sometimes, when a chap doesn't have much, he clings right hard to what he's got. And honest is honest, and there's no two ways about it.

"Why, look, Joe. Seventeen year I worked in that Clarabelle Pit till she shut down, and a good collier too. Seventeen year! And butties I've had by the dozen, and never a man of 'em can ever say that Joe Carraclough kept what wasn't his, nor spoke what wasn't true. Not a man in his Riding can ever call a Carraclough mishonest.

"And when ye've sold a man summat, and ye've taken his brass, and ye've spent it—well, then done's done. That's all. And ye've got to stand by that."

"But Lassie was——"

"Now, Joe! Ye can't alter it, ever. It's done—and happen it's for t' best. No two ways, Joe, she were getting hard to feed. Why, ye wouldn't want Lassie to be going around getting peaked and pined, like some chaps round here keep their tykes. And if ye're fond of her, then just think on it that now she's got lots to eat, and a private kennel, and a good run to herself, and living like a varritable princess, she is. Ain't that best for her?"

"We wouldn't pine her. We've always got lots to eat."

The man blew out his breath, angrily. "Eigh, Joe, nowt pleases thee. Well then, tha might as well have it. Tha'll never see Lassie no more. She run home once too often, so the duke's taken her wi' him up to his place in Scotland, and there she'll stay. So it's good-by and good luck to her, and she'll never come home no more, she won't. Now, I weren't off to tell thee, but there it is, so put it in thy pipe and smoke it, and let's never say a word about it no more—especially in front of thy mother."

The boy stumbled on in the darkness. Then the man halted.

"We ought to be getting back, lad. We left thy mother alone."

He turned the boy about, and then went on, but as if he were talking to himself.

"Tha sees, Joe, women's not like men. They have to stay home and manage best they can, and just spend the time in wishing. And when things don't go right, well, they have to take it out in talk and give a man hell. But it don't mean nowt, really, so tha shouldn't mind when thy mother talks hard.

"Ye just got to learn to be patient and let 'em talk, and just let it go up t' chimney wi' th' smoke."

Then they were quiet, until, over the rise, they saw the lights of the village. Then the boy spoke: "How far away is Scotland, feyther?"

"Nay, lad, it's a long, long road."

"But how far, feyther?"

"I don't know—but it's a longer road than thee or me'll ever walk. Now, lad. Don't fret no more, and try to be a man—and don't plague thy mother no more, wilta?"

Joe Carraclough was right. It is a long road, as they say in the North, from Yorkshire to Scotland. Much too far for a man to walk—or a boy. And though the boy often thought of it, he remembered his father's words on the moor, and he put the thought behind him.

But there is another way of looking at it; and that's the distance from Scotland to Yorkshire. And that is just as far as from Yorkshire to Scotland. A matter of about four hundred miles, it would be, from the Duke of Rudling's place far up in the Highlands, to the village of Holdersby. That would be for a man, who could go fairly straight.

To an animal, how much farther would it be? For a dog can study no maps, read no signposts, ask no directions. It could only go blindly, by instinct, knowing that it must keep on to the south, to the south. It would wander and err, quest and quarter, run into firths and lochs that would send it side-tracking and back-tracking before it could go again on its way—south.

A thousand miles, it would be, going that way—a thousand miles over strange terrain.

There would be moors to cross, and burns to swim. And then those great, long lochs that stretch almost from one side of that dour land to another would bar the way and send a dog questing a hundred miles before it could find a crossing that would allow it to go south.

And, too, there would be rivers to cross, wide rivers like the Forth and the Clyde, the Tweed and the Tyne, where one must go miles to find bridges. And the bridges would be in towns. And in the towns there would be officials—like the one in Lanarkshire. In all his life he had never let a captured dog get away—except one. That one was a gaunt, snarling collie that whirled on him right in the pound itself, and fought and twisted loose to race away down the city street—going south.

But there are also kind people, too; ones knowing and understanding in the ways of dogs. There was an old couple in Durham who found a dog lying exhausted in a ditch one night—lying there with its head to the south. They took that dog into their cottage and warmed it and fed it and nursed it. And because it seemed an understanding, wise dog, they kept it in their home, hoping it would learn to be content. But, as it grew stronger, every afternoon toward four o'clock it would go to the door and whine, and then begin pacing back and forth between the door and the window, back and forth as the animals do in their cages at the zoo.

They tried every wile and every kindness to make it bide

with them, but finally, when the dog began to refuse food, the old people knew what they must do. Because they understood dogs, they opened the door one afternoon and they watched a collie go, not down the road to the right, or to the left, but straight across a field toward the south; going steadily at a trot, as if he knew it still had a long, long road to travel.

Ah, a thousand miles of tor and brae, of shire and moor, of path and road and plowland, of river and stream and burn and brook and beck, of snow and rain and fog and sun, is a long way, even for a human being. But it would seem too far —much, much too far—for any dog to travel blindly and win through.

And yet—and yet—who shall say why, when so many weeks had passed that hope against hope was dying, a boy coming out of school, out of the cloakroom that always smelled of damp wool drying, across the concrete play yard with the black, waxed slides, should turn his eyes to a spot by the school gate from force of five years of habit, and see there a dog? Not a dog, this one, that lifted glad ears above a proud, slim head with its black-and-gold mask; but a dog that lay weakly, trying to lift a head that would no longer lift, trying to wag a tail that was torn and blotched and matted with dirt and burs, and managing to do nothing much except to whine in a weak, happy, crying way as a boy on his knees threw arms about it, and hands touched it that had not touched it for many a day.

Then who shall picture the urgency of a boy, running, awkwardly, with a great dog in his arms running through the village, past the empty mill, past the Labor Exchange, where the men looked up from their deep ponderings on life and the dole? Or who shall describe the high tones of a voice—a boy's voice, calling as he runs up a path: "Mother! Oh, mother! Lassie's come home! Lassie's come home!"

Nor does anyone who ever owned a dog need to be told the sound a man makes as he bends over a dog that has been his for many years; nor how a woman moves quickly, preparing food—which might be the family's condensed milk stirred into warm water; nor how the jowl of a dog is lifted so that raw egg and brandy, bought with precious pence, should be spooned in; nor how bleeding pads are bandaged, tenderly.

That was one day. There was another day when the woman in the cottage sighed with pleasure, for a dog lifted itself to its feet for the first time to stand over a bowl of oatmeal, putting its head down and lapping again and again while its pinched flanks quivered.

And there was another day when the boy realized that, even now, the dog was not to be his again. So the cottage rang again with protests and cries, and a woman shrilling: "Is there never to be no more peace in my house and home?" Long after he was in bed that night the boy heard the rise and fall of the woman's voice, and the steady, reiterative tone of the man's. It went on long after he was asleep.

In the morning the man spoke, not looking at the boy, saying the words as if he had long rehearsed them.

"Thy mother and me have decided upon it that Lassie shall stay here till she's better. Anyhow, nobody could nurse her better than us. But the day that t' duke comes back, then back she goes, too. For she belongs to him, and that's honest, too. Now tha has her for awhile, so be content."

In childhood, "for a while" is such a great stretch of days when seen from one end. It is a terribly short time seen from the other.

The boy knew how short it was that morning as he went to school and saw a motorcar driven by a young woman. And in the car was a gray-thatched, terrible old man, who waved a cane and shouted: "Hi! Hi, there! Damme, lad! You there! Hi!"

Then it was no use running, for the car could go faster than you, and soon it was beside you and the man was saying: "Damme, Philippa, will you make this smelly thing stand still a moment? Hi, lad!"

"Yes, sir."

"You're What's-'is-Name's lad, aren't you?"

"Ma feyther's Joe Carraclough."

"I know. I know. Is he home now?"

"No, sir. He's away to Allerby. A mate spoke for him at the pit and he's gone to see if there's a chance."

"When'll he be back?"

"I don't know. I think about tea."

"Eh, yes. Well, yes. I'll drop round about fivish to see that father of yours. Something important."

It was hard to pretend to listen to lessons. There was only waiting for noon. Then the boy ran home.

"Mother! T' duke is back and he's coming to take Lassie away."

"Eigh, drat my buttons. Never no peace in this house. Is tha sure?"

"Aye. He stopped me. He said tell feyther he'll be round at five. Can't we hide her? Oh, mother."

"Nay, thy feyther——"

"Won't you beg him? Please, please. Beg feyther to——"

"Young Joe, now it's no use. So stop thy teasing! Thy feyther'll not lie. That much I'll give him. Come good, come bad, he'll not lie."

"But just this once, mother. Please beg him, just this once. Just one lie wouldn't hurt him. I'll make it up to him. I will. When I'm growed up, I'll get a job. I'll make money. I'll buy him things—and you, too. I'll buy you both anything you want if you'll only——"

For the first time in his trouble the boy became a child, and the mother, looking over, saw the tears that ran openly down his contorted face. She turned her face to the fire, and there was a pause. Then she spoke.

"Joe, tha mustn't," she said softly. "Tha must learn never to want nothing in life like that. It don't do, lad. Tha mustn't want things bad, like tha wants Lassie."

The boy shook his clenched fists in impatience.

"It ain't that, mother. Ye don't understand. Don't yer see—it ain't me that wants her. It's her that wants us! Tha's wha made her come all them miles. It's her that wants us, so terrible bad!"

The woman turned and stared. It was as if, in that moment, she were seeing this child, this boy, this son of her own, for the first time in many years. She turned her head down toward the table. It was surrender.

"Come and eat, then," she said. "I'll talk to him. I will that, all right. I feel sure he won't lie. But I'll talk to him, all right. I'll talk to Mr. Joe Carraclough. I will indeed."

At five that afternoon, the Duke of Rudling, fuming and muttering, got out of a car at a cottage gate to find a boy barring his way. This was a boy who stood, stubbornly, saying fiercely: "Away wi' thee! Thy tyke's net here!"

"Damme, Philippa, th' lad's touched," the duke said. "He is. He's touched."

Scowling and thumping his stick, the old duke advanced until the boy gave way, backing down the path out of the reach of the waving blackthorn stick.

"Thy tyke's net here," the boy protested.

"What's he saying?" the girl asked.

"Says my dog isn't here. Damme, you going deaf? I'm supposed to be deaf, and I hear him plainly enough. Now, ma lad, what tyke o' mine's net here?"

As he turned to the boy, the duke spoke in broadest Yorkshire, as he did always to the people of the cottages—a habit which the Duchess of Rudling, and many more members of the duke's family, deplored.

"Coom, coom, ma lad. Whet tyke's net here?"

"No tyke o' thine. Us hasn't got it." The words began running faster and faster as the boy backed away from the fearful old man who advanced. "No tyke could have done it. No tyke can come all them miles. It isn't Lassie. It's another one that looks like her. It isn't Lassie!"

"Why, bless ma heart and sowl," the duke puffed. "Where's thy father, ma lad?"

The door behind the boy opened, and a woman's voice spoke.

"If it's Joe Carraclough ye want, he's out in the shed—and been there shut up half the afternoon."

"What's this lad talking about—a dog of mine being here?"

"Nay," the woman snapped quickly. "He didn't say a tyke o' thine was here. He said it wasn't here."

"Well, what dog o' mine isn't here, then?"

The woman swallowed, and looked about as if for help. The duke stood, peering from under his jutting eyebrows. Her answer, truth or lie, was never spoken, for then they heard the rattle of a door opening, and a man making a pursing sound with his lips, as he will when he wants a dog to follow, and then Joe Carraclough's voice said: "This is t' only tyke us has here. Does it look like any dog that belongs to thee?"

With his mouth opening to cry one last protest, the boy turned. And his mouth stayed open. For there he saw his father, Joe Carraclough, the collie fancier, standing with a dog at his heels—a dog that sat at his left heel patiently, as any well-trained dog should do—as Lassie used to do. But this dog was not Lassie. In fact, it was ridiculous to think of it at the same moment as you thought of Lassie.

For where Lassie's skull was aristocratic and slim, this dog's head was clumsy and rough. Where Lassie's ears stood in twin-lapped symmetry, this dog had one ear draggling and the other standing up Alsatian fashion in a way to give any collie breeder the cold shivers. Where Lassie's coat was rich tawny gold, this dog's coat had ugly patches of black; and where Lassie's apron was a billowing stretch of snow-white, this dog had puddles of off-color blue-merle mixture. Besides, Lassie had four white paws, and this one had one paw white, two dirty-brown, and one almost black.

That is the dog they all looked at as Joe Carraclough stood there, having told no lie, having only asked a question. They all stood, waiting the duke's verdict.

But the duke said nothing. He only walked forward, slowly, as if he were seeing a dream. He bent beside the collie, looking with eyes that were as knowing about dogs as any Yorkshireman alive. And those eyes did not waste themselves upon twisted ears, or blotched marking, or rough head. Instead they were looking at a paw that the duke lifted, looking at the underside of the paw, staring intently at five black pads, crossed and recrossed with the scars where thorns had lacerated, and stones had torn.

For a long time the duke stared, and when he got up he did not speak in Yorkshire accents any more. He spoke as a gentleman should, and he said: "Joe Carraclough. I never owned this dog. 'Pon my soul, she's never belonged to me. Never!"

Then he turned and went stumping down the path, thumping his cane and saying: "Bless my soul. Four hundred miles! Damme, wouldn't ha' believed it. Damme—five hundred miles!"

He was at the gate when his granddaughter whispered to him fiercely.

"Of course," he cried. "Mind your own business. Exactly what I came for. Talking about dogs made me forget. Carraclough! Carraclough! What're ye hiding for?"

"I'm still here, sir."

"Ah, there you are. You working?"

"Eigh, now. Working," Joe said. That's the best he could manage.

"Yes, working, working!" The duke fumed.

"Well, now——" Joe began.

Then Mrs. Carraclough came to his rescue, as a good house-wife in Yorkshire will.

"Why, Joe's got three or four things that he's been con-sidering," she said, with proper display of pride. "But he hasn't quite said yes or no to any of them yet."

"Then say no, quick," the old man puffed. "Had to sack Hynes. Didn't know a dog from a drunken filly. Should ha' known all along no damn Londoner could handle dogs fit for Yorkshire taste. How much, Carraclough?"

"Well, now," Joe began.

"Seven pounds a week, and worth every penny," Mrs. Carraclough chipped in. "One o' them other offers may come up to eight," she lied, expertly. For there's always a certain amount of lying to be done in life, and when a woman's mar-ried to a man who has made a lifelong cult of being honest, then she's got to learn to do the lying for two.

"Five," roared the duke—who, after all, was a Yorkshire-man, and couldn't help being a bit sharp about things that pertained to money.

"Six," said Mrs. Carraclough.

"Five pound ten," bargained the duke, cannily.

"Done," said Mrs. Carraclough, who would have been will-ing to settle for three pounds in the first place. "But, o' course, us gets the cottage too."

"All right," puffed the duke. "Five pounds ten and the cottage. Begin Monday. But—on one condition. Carraclough, you can live on my land, but I won't have that thick-skulled, screw-lugged, gay-tailed eyesore of a misshapen mongrel on my property. Now never let me see her again. You'll get rid of her?"

He waited, and Joe fumbled for words. But it was the boy

who answered, happily, gaily: "Oh, no, sir. She'll be waiting at school for me most o' the time. And, anyway, in a day or so we'll have her fixed up and coped up so's ye'd never, never recognize her."

"I don't doubt that," puffed the duke, as he went to the car. "I don't doubt ye could do just exactly that."

It was a long time afterward, in the car, that the girl said: "Don't sit there like a lion on the Nelson column. And I thought you were supposed to be a hard man."

"Fiddlesticks, m'dear. I'm a ruthless realist. For five years I've sworn I'd have that dog by hook or crook, and now, egad, at last I've got her."

"Pooh! You had to buy the man before you could get his dog."

"Well, perhaps that's not the worst part of the bargain."

BRET HARTE

A Yellow Dog

I NEVER knew why in the Western States of America a
yellow dog should be proverbially considered the acme of
canine degradation and incompetency, nor why the possession
of one should seriously affect the social standing of its pos-
sessor. But the fact being established, I think we accepted it
at Rattlers Ridge without question. The matter of ownership
was more difficult to settle; and although the dog I have in
my mind at the present writing attached himself impartially
and equally to everyone in camp, no one ventured to exclu-
sively claim him; while, after the perpetration of any canine
atrocity, everybody repudiated him with indecent haste.

"Well, I can swear he hasn't been near our shanty for
weeks," or the retort, "He was last seen comin' out of *your*
cabin," expressed the eagerness with which Rattlers Ridge
washed its hands of any responsibility. Yet he was by no
means a common dog, nor even an unhandsome dog; and it
was a singular fact that his severest critics vied with each
other in narrating instances of his sagacity, insight, and agility
which they themselves had witnessed.

He had been seen crossing the "flume" that spanned Grizzly Cañon at a height of nine hundred feet, on a plank six inches wide. He had tumbled down the "shoot" to the South Fork, a thousand feet below, and was found sitting on the riverbank "without a scratch, 'cept that he was lazily givin' himself with his off hind paw." He had been forgotten in a snowdrift on a Sierran shelf, and had come home in the early spring with the conceited complacency of an Alpine traveler and a plumpness alleged to have been the result of an exclusive diet of buried mail bags and their contents. He was generally believed to read the advance election posters, and disappear a day or two before the candidates and the brass band—which he hated—came to the Ridge. He was suspected of having overlooked Colonel Johnson's hand at poker, and of having conveyed to the Colonel's adversary, by a succession of barks, the danger of betting against four kings.

While these statements were supplied by wholly unsupported witnesses, it was a very human weakness of Rattlers Ridge that the responsibility of corroboration was passed to the dog himself, and *he* was looked upon as a consummate liar.

"Snoopin' round yere, and *callin'* yourself a poker sharp, are ye! Scoot, you yaller pizin!" was a common adjuration whenever the unfortunate animal intruded upon a card party. "Ef thar was a spark, an *atom* of truth in *that dog*, I'd believe my own eyes that I saw him sittin' up and trying to magnetize a jay bird off a tree. But wot are ye goin' to do with a yaller equivocator like that?"

I have said that he was yellow—or, to use the ordinary expression, "yaller." Indeed, I am inclined to believe that much of the ignominy attached to the epithet lay in this favorite pronunciation. Men who habitually spoke of a "*yellow* bird," a "*yellow*-hammer," a "*yellow* leaf," always alluded to him as a "*yaller* dog."

He certainly *was* yellow. After a bath—usually compulsory —he presented a decided gamboge streak down his back, from the top of his forehead to the stump of his tail, fading in his sides and flank to a delicate straw color. His breast, legs, and feet—when not reddened by "slumgullion," in which he was fond of wading—were white. A few attempts at ornamental decoration from the India-ink pot of the storekeeper failed, partly through the yellow dog's excessive agility, which would never give the paint time to dry on him, and partly through his success in transferring his markings to the trousers and blankets of the camp.

The size and shape of his tail—which had been cut off before his introduction to Rattlers Ridge—were favorite sources of speculation to the miners, as determining both his breed and his moral responsibility in coming into camp in that defective condition. There was a general opinion that he couldn't have looked worse with a tail, and its removal was therefore a gratuitous effrontery.

His best feature was his eyes, which were a lustrous Van-dyke brown, and sparkling with intelligence; but here again he suffered from evolution through environment, and their original trustful openness was marred by the experience of watching for flying stones, sods, and passing kicks from the rear, so that the pupils were continually reverting to the outer angle of the eyelid.

Nevertheless, none of these characteristics decided the vexed question of his *breed*. His speed and scent pointed to a "hound," and it is related that on one occasion he was laid on the trail of a wildcat with such success that he followed it apparently out of the State, returning at the end of two weeks footsore, but blandly contented.

Attaching himself to a prospecting party, he was sent under the same belief, "into the brush" to drive off a bear, who was supposed to be haunting the campfire. He returned in a few minutes *with* the bear, *driving it into* the unarmed circle and scattering the whole party. After this the theory of his being a hunting dog was abandoned. Yet it was said—on the usual uncorroborated evidence—that he had "put up" a quail; and his qualities as a retriever were for a long time accepted, until, during a shooting expedition for wild ducks, it was discovered that the one he had brought back had never been shot, and the party were obliged to compound damages with an adjacent settler.

His fondness for paddling in the ditches and "slumgullion" at one time suggested a water spaniel. He could swim, and would occasionally bring out of the river sticks and pieces of bark that had been thrown in; but as *he* always had to be thrown in with them, and was a good-sized dog, his aquatic reputation faded also. He remained simply "a yaller dog." What more could be said? His actual name was "Bones"— given to him, no doubt, through the provincial custom of confounding the occupation of the individual with his quality, for which it was pointed out precedent could be found in some old English family names.

But if Bones generally exhibited no preference for any particular individual in camp, he always made an exception in favor of drunkards. Even an ordinary roistering bacchanalian party brought him out from under a tree or a shed in the keenest satisfaction. He would accompany them through the long straggling street of the settlement, barking his delight at every step or misstep of the revelers, and exhibiting none of that mistrust of eye which marked his attendance upon the sane and the respectable. He accepted even their uncouth play without a snarl or a yelp, hypocritically pretending even to like it; and I conscientiously believe would have allowed a tin can to be attached to his tail if the hand that tied it on were only unsteady, and the voice that bade him "lie still" were husky with liquor. He would "see" the party cheerfully into a saloon, wait outside the door—his tongue fairly lolling from his mouth in enjoyment—until they reappeared, permit them even to tumble over him with pleasure, and then gambol away before them, heedless of awkwardly projected stones and epithets. He would afterward accompany them separately home, or lie with them at crossroads until they were assisted to their cabins. Then he would trot rakishly to his own haunt by the saloon stove, with the slightly conscious air of having been a bad dog, yet of having had a good time.

We never could satisfy ourselves whether his enjoyment arose from some merely selfish conviction that he was more *secure* with the physically and mentally incompetent, from some active sympathy with active wickedness, or from a grim sense of his own mental superiority at such moments. But the general belief leant toward his kindred sympathy as a "yaller dog" with all that was disreputable. And this was supported by another very singular canine manifestation—the "sincere flattery" of simulation or imitation.

"Uncle Billy" Riley for a short time enjoyed the position of being the camp drunkard, and at once became an object of Bones' greatest solicitude. He not only accompanied him everywhere, curled at his feet or head according to Uncle Billy's attitude at the moment, but, it was noticed, began presently to undergo a singular alteration in his own habits and appearance. From being an active, tireless scout and forager, a bold and unovertakable marauder, he became lazy and apathetic; allowed gophers to burrow under him without endeavoring to undermine the settlement in his frantic endeavors to dig them out, permitted squirrels to flash their tails at him a hundred yards away, forgot his usual caches, and left his favorite bones unburied and bleaching in the sun. His eyes grew dull, his coat lusterless, in proportion as his companion became blear-eyed and ragged; in running, his usual arrowlike directness began to deviate, and it was not unusual to meet the pair together, zigzagging up the hill. Indeed, Uncle Billy's condition could be predetermined by Bones' appearance at times when his temporary master was invisible. "The old man must have an awful jag on today," was casually remarked when an extra fluffiness and imbecility was noticeable in the passing Bones. At first it was believed that he drank also, but when careful investigation proved this hypothesis untenable, he was freely called a "derned time-servin', yaller hypocrite." Not a few advanced the opinion that if Bones did not actually lead Uncle Billy astray, he at least "slavered him over and coddled him until the old man got conceited in his wickedness." This undoubtedly led to a compulsory divorce between them, and Uncle Billy was happily dispatched to a neighboring town and a doctor.

Bones seemed to miss him greatly, ran away for two days, and was supposed to have visited him, to have been shocked at his convalescence, and to have been "cut" by Uncle Billy in his reformed character; and he returned to his old active life again, and buried his past with his forgotten bones. It was said that he was afterward detected in trying to lead an intoxicated tramp into camp after the methods employed by a blind man's dog, but was discovered in time by the—of course —uncorroborated narrator.

I should be tempted to leave him thus in his original and picturesque sin, but the same veracity which compelled me to transcribe his faults and iniquities obliges me to describe his ultimate and somewhat monotonous reformation, which came from no fault of his own.

It was a joyous day at Rattlers Ridge that was equally the advent of his change of heart and the first stagecoach that had been induced to diverge from the highroad and stop regularly at our settlement. Flags were flying from the post office and Polka saloon, and Bones was flying before the brass band that he detested, when the sweetest girl in the county—Pinkey Preston—daughter of the county judge and hopelessly beloved by all Rattlers Ridge, stepped from the coach which she had glorified by occupying as an invited guest.

"What makes him run away?" she asked quickly, opening her lovely eyes in a possibly innocent wonder that anything could be found to run away from her.

"He don't like the brass band," we explained eagerly.

"How funny," murmured the girl; "is it as out of tune as all that?"

This irresistible witticism alone would have been enough to satisfy us—we did nothing but repeat it to each other all the next day—but we were positively transported when we saw her suddenly gather her dainty skirts in one hand and trip off through the red dust toward Bones, who, with his eyes over his yellow shoulder, had halted in the road, and half-turned in mingled disgust and rage at the spectacle of the descending trombone. We held our breath as she approached him. Would Bones evade her as he did us at such moments, or would he save our reputation, and consent, for the moment, to accept her as a new kind of inebriate? She came nearer; he saw her; he began to slowly quiver with excitement—his stump of a tail vibrating with such rapidity that the loss of the missing portion was scarcely noticeable. Suddenly she stopped before him, took his yellow head between her little hands, lifted it, and looked down in his handsome brown eyes with her two lovely blue ones. What passed between them in that magnetic glance no one ever knew. She returned with him; said to him casually: "We're not afraid of brass bands, are we?" to which he apparently acquiesced, at least stifling his disgust of them while he was near her—which was nearly all the time.

During the speechmaking her gloved hand and his yellow head were always near together, and at the crowning cere-mony—her public checking of Yuba Bill's "waybill" on behalf of the township, with a gold pencil presented to her by the Stage Company—Bones' joy, far from knowing no bounds, seemed to know nothing but them, and he witnessed it appar-ently in the air. No one dared to interfere. For the first time a local pride in Bones sprang up in our hearts—and we lied to each other in his praises openly and shamelessly.

Then the time came for parting. We were standing by the door of the coach, hats in hand, as Miss Pinkey was about to

"He don't like the brass band."

step into it; Bones was waiting by her side, confidently looking into the interior, and apparently selecting his own seat on
the lap of Judge Preston in the corner, when Miss Pinkey held
up the sweetest of admonitory fingers. Then, taking his head
between her two hands, she again looked into his brimming
eyes, and said, simply, "*Good* dog," with the gentlest of em-
phasis on the adjective, and popped into the coach.

The six bay horses started as one, the gorgeous green and
gold vehicle bounded forward, the red dust rose behind, and
the yellow dog danced in and out of it to the very outskirts of
the settlement. And then he soberly returned.

A day or two later he was missed—but the fact was afterward known that he was at Spring Valley, the county town
where Miss Preston lived, and he was forgiven. A week afterward he was missed again, but this time for a longer period,
and then a pathetic letter arrived from Sacramento for the
storekeeper's wife.

"Would you mind," wrote Miss Pinkey Preston, "asking
some of your boys to come over here to Sacramento and bring
back Bones? I don't mind having the dear dog walk out with
me at Spring Valley, where everyone knows me; but here he
does make one so noticeable, on account of *his color*. I've got
scarcely a frock that he agrees with. He don't go with my
pink muslin, and that lovely buff tint he makes three shades
lighter. You know yellow is *so* trying."

A consultation was quickly held by the whole settlement,
and a deputation sent to Sacramento to relieve the unfortunate
girl. We were all quite indignant with Bones—but, oddly
enough, I think it was greatly tempered with our new pride
in him. While he was with us alone, his peculiarities had been
scarcely appreciated, but the recurrent phrase "that yellow
dog that they keep at the Rattlers" gave us a mysterious im-
portance along the countryside, as if we had secured a
"mascot" in some zoological curiosity.

This was further indicated by a singular occurrence. A new

church had been built at the crossroads, and an eminent divine had come from San Francisco to preach the opening sermon. After a careful examination of the camp's wardrobe, and some felicitous exchange of apparel, a few of us were deputed to represent "Rattlers" at the Sunday service. In our white ducks, straw hats, and flannel blouses, we were sufficiently picturesque and distinctive as "honest miners" to be shown off in one of the front pews.

Seated near the prettiest girls, who offered us their hymn books—in the cleanly odor of fresh pine shavings, and ironed muslin, and blown over by the spices of our own woods through the open windows, a deep sense of the abiding peace of Christian communion settled upon us. At this supreme moment someone murmured in an awestricken whisper:

"*Will* you look at Bones?"

We looked. Bones had entered the church and gone up in the gallery through a pardonable ignorance and modesty; but, perceiving his mistake, was now calmly walking along the gallery rail before the astounded worshipers. Reaching the end, he paused for a moment, and carelessly looked down. It was about fifteen feet to the floor below—the simplest jump in the world for the mountain-bred Bones. Daintily, gingerly, lazily, and yet with a conceited airiness of manner, as if, humanly speaking, he had one leg in his pocket and were doing it on three, he cleared the distance, dropping just in front of the chancel, without a sound, turned himself around three times, and then lay comfortably down.

Three deacons were instantly in the aisle, coming up before the eminent divine, who, we fancied, wore a restrained smile. We heard the hurried whispers: "Belongs to them." "Quite a local institution here, you know." "Don't like to offend sensibilities"; and the minister's prompt "By no means," as he went on with his service.

A short month ago we would have repudiated Bones; today we sat there in slightly supercilious attitudes, as if to indicate

that any affront offered to Bones would be an insult to ourselves, and followed by our instantaneous withdrawal in a
body.

All went well, however, until the minister, lifting the large
Bible from the communion table and holding it in both hands
before him, walked toward a reading stand by the altar rails.
Bones uttered a distinct growl. The minister stopped.

We, and we alone, comprehended in a flash the whole situation. The Bible was nearly the size and shape of one of those
soft clods of sod which we were in the playful habit of launch-
ing at Bones when he lay half-asleep in the sun, in order to
see him cleverly evade it.

We held our breath. What was to be done? But the opportunity belonged to our leader, Jeff Briggs—a confoundedly
good-looking fellow, with the golden mustache of a northern
viking and the curls of an Apollo. Secure in his beauty and
bland in his self-conceit, he rose from the pew, and stepped
before the chancel rails.

"I would wait a moment, if I were you, sir," he said, re-
spectfully, "and you will see that he will go out quietly."

"What is wrong?" whispered the minister in some
concern.

"He thinks you are going to heave that book at him, sir,
without giving him a fair show, as we do."

The minister looked perplexed, but remained motionless,
with the book in his hands. Bones arose, walked halfway down
the aisle, and vanished like a yellow flash!

With this justification of his reputation, Bones disappeared
for a week. At the end of that time we received a polite note
from Judge Preston, saying that the dog had become quite
domiciled in their house, and begged that the camp, without
yielding up their valuable *property* in him, would allow him
to remain at Spring Valley for an indefinite time; that both
the judge and his daughter—with whom Bones was already
an old friend—would be glad if the members of the camp

would visit their old favorite whenever they desired, to assure themselves that he was well cared for.

I am afraid that the bait thus ingenuously thrown out had a good deal to do with our ultimate yielding. However, the reports of those who visited Bones were wonderful and marvelous. He was residing there in state, lying on rugs in the drawing-room, coiled up under the judicial desk in the judge's study, sleeping regularly on the mat outside Miss Pinkey's bedroom door, or lazily snapping at flies on the judge's lawn.

"He's as yaller as ever," said one of our informants, "but it don't somehow seem to be the same back that we used to break clods over in the old time, just to see him scoot out of the dust."

And now I must record a fact which I am aware all lovers of dogs will indignantly deny, and which will be furiously bayed at by every faithful hound since the day of Ulysses. Bones not only *forgot*, but absolutely *cut us!* Those who called upon the judge in "store clothes" he would perhaps casually notice, but he would sniff at them as if detecting and resenting them under their superficial exterior. The rest he simply paid no attention to. The more familiar term of "Bonesy"—formerly applied to him, as in our rare moments of endearment—produced no response. This pained, I think, some of the more youthful of us; but, through some strange human weakness, it also increased the camp's respect for him. Nevertheless, we spoke of him familiarly to strangers at the very moment he ignored us. I am afraid that we also took some pains to point out that he was getting fat and unwieldy, and losing his elasticity, implying covertly that his choice was a mistake and his life a failure.

A year after, he died, in the odor of sanctity and respectability, being found one morning coiled up and stiff on the mat outside Miss Pinkey's door. When the news was conveyed to us, we asked permission, the camp being in a prosperous condition, to erect a stone over his grave. But when it came to the inscription we could only think of the two words murmured to him by Miss Pinkey, which we always believe effected his conversion:

"*Good* Dog!"

JOHN MUIR

An Adventure with a Dog

In the summer of 1880 I set out from Fort Wrangel in a canoe, with the Rev. S. H. Young, my former companion, and a crew of Indians, to continue the exploration of the icy region of southeastern Alaska, begun in the fall of 1879. After the necessary provisions, blankets, etc., had been collected and stowed away, and the Indians were in their places ready to dip their paddles, while a crowd of their friends were looking down from the wharf to bid them good-by and good luck, Mr. Young, for whom we were waiting, at length came aboard, followed by a little black dog that immediately made himself at home by curling up in a hollow among the baggage. I like dogs, but this one seemed so small, dull, and worthless that I objected to his going, and asked the missionary why he was taking him. "Such a helpless wisp of hair will only be in the way," I said; "you had better pass him up to one of the Indian boys on the wharf, to be taken home to play with the children. This trip is not likely to be a good one for toy dogs. He will be rained on and snowed on for weeks, and will require care like a baby." But the missionary assured me that he would be no trouble at all; that he was a perfect wonder of a dog—could endure cold and hunger like a polar bear, could swim like a seal, and was wondrous wise, etc., making out a list of virtues likely to make him the most interesting of the company.

Nobody could hope to unravel the lines of his ancestry. He was short-legged, bunchy-bodied, and almost featureless—something like a muskrat. Though smooth, his hair was long and silky, so that when the wind was at his back it ruffled, making him look shaggy. At first sight his only noticeable feature was his showy tail, which was about as shady and airy as a squirrel's, and was carried curling forward nearly to his ears. On closer inspection you might see his thin, sensitive ears and his keen dark eyes with cunning tan spots. Mr. Young told me that when the dog was about the size of a woodrat he was presented to his wife by an Irish prospector at Sitka, and that when he arrived at Fort Wrangel he was adopted by the Stickeen Indians as a sort of new good-luck totem, and named "Stickeen" for the tribe, with whom he became a favorite. On our trip he soon proved himself a queer character—odd, concealed, independent, keeping invincibly quiet, and doing many inexplicable things that piqued my curiosity. Sailing week after week through the long, intricate channels and inlets among the innumerable islands and mountains of the coast, he spent the dull days in sluggish ease, motionless, and apparently as unobserving as a hibernating marmot. But I discovered that somehow he always knew what was going forward. When the Indians were about to shoot at ducks or seals, or when anything interesting was to be seen along the shore, he would rest his chin on the edge of the canoe and calmly look out. When he heard us talking about making a landing, he roused himself to see what sort of place we were coming to, and made ready to jump overboard and swim ashore as soon as the canoe neared the beach. Then, with a vigorous shake to get rid of the brine in his hair, he went into the woods to hunt small game. But though always the first out of the canoe, he was always the last to get into it. When we were ready to start he could never be found, and refused to come to our call. We soon found out, however, that though we could not see him at such times, he saw us, and from the cover of the briers and huckleberry-bushes in the fringe of the woods was watching the canoe with wary eye. For as soon as we were fairly off, he came trotting down the beach, plunged into the surf, and swam after us, knowing well that we would cease rowing and take him in. When the contrary little vagabond came alongside, he was lifted by the neck, held at arm's length a moment to drip, and dropped aboard. We tried to cure him of this trick by compelling him to swim farther before stopping for him; but this did no good: the longer the swim, the better he seemed to like it.

Though capable of most spacious idleness, he was always ready for excursions or adventures of any sort. When the Indians went into the woods for a deer, Stickeen was sure to be at their heels, provided I had not yet left camp. For though I never carried a gun, he always followed me, forsaking the hunting Indians, and even his master, to share my wanderings. The days that were too stormy for sailing I spent in the woods, or on the mountains or glaciers, wherever I chanced to be; and Stickeen always insisted on following me, gliding through the dripping huckleberry-bushes and prickly *Panax* and *Rubus* tangles like a fox, scarce stirring their close-set branches, wading and wallowing through snow, swimming ice-cold streams, jumping logs and rocks and the crusty hummocks and crevasses of glaciers with the patience and endurance of a determined mountaineer, never tiring or getting discouraged. Once he followed me over a glacier the surface of which was so rough that it cut his feet until every step was marked with blood; but he trotted on with Indian fortitude until I noticed his pain and, taking pity on him, made him a set of moccasins out of a handkerchief. But he never asked help or made any complaint, as if, like a philosopher, he had learned that without hard work and suffering there could be no pleasure worth having.

Yet nobody knew what Stickeen was good for. He seemed to meet danger and hardships without reason, insisted on having his own way, never obeyed an order, and the hunters could never set him on anything against his will, or make him fetch anything that was shot. I tried hard to make his acquaintance, guessing there must be something in him; but he was as cold as a glacier, and about as invulnerable to fun, though his master assured me that he played at home, and in some measure conformed to the usages of civilization. His equanimity was so immovable it seemed due to unfeeling ignorance. Let the weather blow and roar, he was as tranquil as a stone; and no matter what advances you made, scarce a glance or a tail-wag would you get for your pains. No superannuated mastiff or bulldog grown old in office surpassed this soft midget in stoic dignity. He sometimes reminded me of those plump, squat, unshakable cacti of the Arizona deserts that give no sign of feeling. A true child of the wilderness, holding the even tenor of his hidden life with the silence and serenity of nature, he never displayed a trace of the elfish vivacity and fun of the terriers and collies that we all know, nor of their touching affection and devotion. Like children, most small dogs beg to be loved and allowed to love, but Stickeen seemed a very Diogenes, asking only to be let alone. He seemed neither old nor young. His strength lay in his eyes. They looked as old as the hills, and as young and as wild. I never tired looking into them. It was like looking into a landscape; but they were small and rather deep-set, and had no explaining puckers around them to give out particulars. I was accustomed to look into the faces of plants and animals, and I watched the little sphinx more and more keenly as an interesting study. But there is no estimating the wit and wisdom concealed and latent in our lower fellow-mortals until made manifest by profound experiences; for it is by suffering that dogs as well as saints are developed and made perfect.

After we had explored the glaciers of the Sumdum and Tahkoo inlets, we sailed through Stephen's Passage into Lynn Canal, and thence through Icy Strait into Cross Sound, looking for unexplored inlets leading toward the ice-fountains of the Fairweather Range. While the tide was in our favor in Cross Sound we were accompanied by a fleet of icebergs drifting out to the ocean from Glacier Bay. Slowly we crawled around Vancouver's Point, Wimbleton, our frail canoe tossed like a feather on the massive swells coming in past Cape Spenser. For miles the Sound is bounded by precipitous cliffs which looked terribly stern in gloomy weather. Had our canoe been crushed or upset, we could have gained no landing here; for the cliffs, as high as those of Yosemite, sink perfectly sheer into deep water. Eagerly we scanned the immense wall on the north side for the first sign of an opening, all of us anxious except Stickeen, who dozed in peace or gazed dreamily at the tremendous precipices when he heard us talking about them. At length we discovered the entrance of what is now called Taylor Bay, and about five o'clock reached the head of it, and encamped near the front of a large glacier which extends as an abrupt barrier all the way across from wall to wall of the inlet, a distance of three or four miles.

On first observation the glacier presented some unusual features, and that night I planned a grand excursion for the morrow. I awoke early, called not only by the glacier, but also by a storm. Rain, mixed with trailing films of scud and the ragged, drawn-out nether surfaces of gray clouds, filled the inlet, and was sweeping forward in a thick, passionate, horizontal flood, as if it were all passing over the country instead of falling on it. Everything was streaming with life and motion—woods, rocks, waters, and the sky. The main perennial streams were booming, and hundreds of new ones, born of the rain, were descending in gray and white cascades on each side of the inlet, fairly streaking their rocky slopes, and roaring like the sea. I had intended making a cup of coffee before starting, but when I heard the storm I made haste to join it; for in storms nature has always something extra fine to show us, and if we have wit to keep in right relations with them the danger is no more than in home-keeping, and we can go with them rejoicing, sharing their enthusiasm, and chanting with the old Norsemen, "The blast of the tempest aids our oars; the hurricane is our servant, and drives us whither we wish to go." So I took my ice-ax, buttoned my coat, put a piece of bread in my pocket, and set out. Mr. Young and the Indians were asleep, and so, I hoped, was Stickeen; but I had not gone a dozen rods before he left his warm bed in the tent, and came boring through the blast after me. That a man should welcome storms for their exhilarating music and motion, and go forth to see God making landscapes, is reasonable enough; but what fascination could there be in dismal weather for this poor, feeble wisp of a dog, so pathetically small? Anyhow, on he came, breakfastless, through the choking blast. I stopped, turned my back to the wind, and gave him a good, dissuasive talk. "Now don't," I said, shouting to make myself heard in the storm—"now don't, Stickeen. What has got into your queer noddle now? You must be daft. This wild day has nothing for you. Go back to camp and keep warm. There is no game abroad—nothing but weather. Not a foot or wing is stirring. Wait and get a good breakfast with your master, and be sensible for once. I can't feed you or carry you, and this storm will kill you." But nature, it seems, was at the bottom of the affair; and she gains her ends with dogs as well as with men, making us do as she likes, driving us on her ways, however rough. So after ordering him back again and again to ease my conscience, I saw that he was not to be shaken off; as well might the earth try to shake off the moon. I had once led his master into trouble, when he fell on one of the topmost jags of a mountain, and dislocated his arms. Now the turn of his humble companion was coming. The dog just stood there in the wind, drenched and blinking, saying doggedly, "Where thou goest I will go." So I told him to come on, if he must, and gave him a piece of the bread I had put in my pocket for breakfast. Then we pushed on in company, and thus began the most memorable of all my wild days.

The level flood, driving straight in our faces, thrashed and washed us wildly until we got into the shelter of the trees and ice-cliffs on the east side of the glacier, where we rested and listened and looked on in comfort. The exploration of the glacier was my main object, but the wind was too high to allow excursions over its open surface, where one might be dangerously shoved while balancing for a jump on the brink of a crevasse. In the meantime the storm was a fine study. Here the end of the glacier, descending over an abrupt swell of resisting rock about five hundred feet high, leans forward and falls in majestic ice-cascades. And as the storm came down the glacier from the north, Stickeen and I were beneath the main current of the blast, while favorably located to see and hear it. A broad torrent, draining the side of the glacier, now swollen by scores of new streams from the mountains, was rolling boulders along its rocky channel between the glacier and the woods with thudding, bumping, muffled sounds, rushing toward the bay with tremendous energy, as if in haste to get out of the mountains, the waters above and beneath calling to each other, and all to the ocean, their home. Looking southward from our shelter, we had this great torrent on our left, with mossy woods on the mountain slope above it, the glacier on our right, the wild, cascading portion of it forming a multitude of towers, spires, and flat-topped battlements seen through the trees, and smooth gray gloom ahead. I tried to draw the marvelous scene in my note-book, but the rain fell on my page in spite of all that I could do to shelter it, and the sketch seemed miserably defective.

When the wind began to abate I traced the east side of the

glacier. All the trees standing on the edge of the woods were barked and bruised, showing high ice-mark in a very telling way, while tens of thousands of those that had stood for centuries on the bank of the glacier farther out lay crushed and being crushed. In many places I could see, down fifty feet or so beneath, the margin of the glacier mill, where trunks from one to two feet in diameter were being ground to pulp against outstanding rock-ribs and bosses of the bank. About three miles above the front of the glacier, I climbed to the surface of it by means of ax-steps, made easy for Stickeen; and as far as the eye could reach, the level, or nearly level, glacier stretched away indefinitely beneath the gray sky, a seemingly boundless prairie of ice. The rain continued, which I did not mind; but a tendency to fogginess in the drooping clouds made me hesitate about venturing far from land. No trace of the west shore was visible, and in case the misty clouds should settle, or the wind again become violent, I feared getting caught in a tangle of crevasses. Lingering undecided, watching the weather, I sauntered about on the crystal sea. For a mile or two out I found the ice remarkably safe. The marginal crevasses were mostly narrow, while the few wider ones were easily avoided by passing around them, and the clouds began to open here and there. Thus encouraged, I at last pushed out for the other side; for nature can make us do anything she likes, luring us along appointed ways for the fulfilment of her plans. At first we made rapid progress, and the sky was not very threatening, while I took bearings occasionally with a pocket-compass, to enable me to retrace my way more surely in case the storm should become blinding; but the structure-lines of the ice were my main guide. Toward the west side we came to a closely crevassed section, in which we had to make long, narrow tacks and doublings, tracing the edges of tremendous longitudinal crevasses, many of which were from twenty to thirty feet wide, and perhaps a thousand feet deep, beautiful and awful. In working a way through them I was severely cautious, but Stickeen came on as unhesitatingly as the flying clouds. Any crevasse that I could jump he would leap without so much as halting to examine it. The weather was bright and dark, with quick flashes of summer and winter close together. When the clouds opened and the sun shone, the glacier was seen from shore to shore, with a bright array of encompassing mountains partly revealed, wearing the clouds as garments, black in the middle, burning on the edges, and the whole icy prairie seemed to burst into a bloom of iris colors from myriads of crystals. Then suddenly all the glorious show would be again smothered in gloom. But Stickeen seemed to care for none of these things, bright or dark, nor for the beautiful wells filled to the brim with water so pure that it was nearly invisible, the rumbling, grinding moulins, or the quick-flashing, glinting, swirling streams in frictionless channels of living ice. Nothing seemed novel to him. He showed neither caution nor curiosity. His courage was so unwavering that it seemed due to dullness of perception, as if he were only blindly bold; and I warned him that he might slip or fall short. His bunchy body seemed all one skipping muscle, and his peg legs appeared to be jointed only at the top.

We gained the west shore in about three hours, the width of the glacier here being about seven miles. Then I pushed northward, in order to see as far back as possible into the fountains of the Fairweather Mountains, in case the clouds should rise. The walking was easy along the margin of the forest, which, of course, like that on the other side, had been invaded and crushed by the swollen glacier. In an hour we rounded a massive headland and came suddenly on another outlet of the glacier, which, in the form of a wild ice-cascade, was pouring over the rim of the main basin toward the ocean with the volume of a thousand Niagaras. The surface was broken into a multitude of sharp blades and pinnacles leaning forward, something like the updashing waves of a flood of water descending a rugged channel. But these ice-waves were many times higher than those of river cataracts, and to all appearance motionless. It was a dazzling white torrent two miles wide, flowing between high banks black with trees. Tracing its left bank three or four miles, I found that it discharged into a fresh-water lake, filling it with icebergs.

I would gladly have followed the outlet, but the day was waning, and we had to make haste on the return trip to get off the ice before dark. When we were about two miles from the west shore the clouds dropped misty fringes, and snow soon began to fly. Then I began to feel anxiety as to finding a way in the storm through the intricate net-work of crevasses which we had entered. Stickeen showed no fear. He was still the same silent, sufficient, uncomplaining Indian philosopher. When the storm-darkness fell he kept close behind me. The snow warned us to make haste, but at the same time hid our way. At rare intervals the clouds thinned, and mountains, looming in the gloom, frowned and quickly vanished. I pushed on as best I could, jumping innumerable crevasses, and for every hundred rods or so of direct advance traveling a mile in doubling up and down in the turmoil of chasms and dislocated masses of ice. After an hour or two of this work we came to a series of longitudinal crevasses of appalling width, like immense furrows. These I traced with firm nerve, excited and strengthened by the danger, making wide jumps, poising cautiously on the dizzy edges after cutting hollows for my feet before making the spring, to avoid slipping or any uncertainty on the farther sides, where only one trial is granted— exercise at once frightful and inspiring. Stickeen flirted across every gap I jumped, seemingly without effort. Many a mile we thus traveled, mostly up and down, making but little real headway in crossing, most of the time running instead of walking, as the danger of spending the night on the glacier became threatening. No doubt we could have weathered the storm for one night, and I faced the chance of being compelled to do so; but we were hungry and wet, and the north wind was thick with snow and bitterly cold, and of course that night would have seemed a long one. Stickeen gave me no concern. He was still the wonderful, inscrutable philosopher, ready for anything. I could not see far enough to judge in which direction the best route lay, and had simply to grope my way in the snow-choked air and ice. Again and again I was put to my mettle, but Stickeen followed easily, his nerves growing more unflinching as the dangers thickened; so it always is with mountaineers.

At length our way was barred by a very wide and straight crevasse, which I traced rapidly northward a mile or so without finding a crossing or hope of one, then southward down the glacier about as far, to where it united with another crevasse. In all this distance of perhaps two miles there was only one place where I could possibly jump it; but the width of this jump was nearly the utmost I dared attempt, while the danger of slipping on the farther side was so great that I was loath to try it. Furthermore, the side I was on was about a foot higher than the other, and even with this advantage it seemed dangerously wide. One is liable to underestimate the width of crevasses where the magnitudes in general are great. I therefore measured this one again and again, until satisfied that I could jump it if necessary, but that in case I should be compelled to jump back to the higher side, I might fail. Now a cautious mountaineer seldom takes a step on unknown ground which seems at all dangerous, that he cannot retrace in case he should be stopped by unseen obstacles ahead. This is the rule of mountaineers who live long; and though in haste, I compelled myself to sit down and deliberate before I broke it. Retracing my devious path in imagination, as if it were drawn on a chart, I saw that I was recrossing the glacier a mile or two farther up-stream, and was entangled in a section I had not before seen. Should I risk this dangerous jump, or try to regain the woods on the west shore, make a fire, and have only hunger to endure while waiting for a new day? I had already crossed so broad a tangle of dangerous ice that I saw it would be difficult to get back to the woods through the storm; while the ice just beyond the present barrier seemed more promising, and the east shore was now perhaps about as near as the west. I was therefore eager to go on; but this wide jump was a tremendous obstacle. At length, because of the dangers already behind me, I determined to venture against those that might be ahead, jumped, and landed well, but with so little to spare that I more than ever dreaded being compelled to take that jump back from the lower side. Stickeen followed, making nothing of it. But within a distance of a few hundred yards we were stopped again by the widest crevasse yet encountered. Of course I made haste to explore it, hoping all might yet be well. About three fourths of a mile up-stream it united with the one we had just crossed, as I feared it would. Then, tracing it down, I found it joined the other great crevasse at the lower end, maintaining a width of forty to fifty feet. We were on an island about two miles long and from one hundred to three hundred yards wide, with two barely possible ways of escape—one by the way we came, the other by an almost inaccessible sliver-bridge that crossed the larger crevasse from near the middle of the island. After tracing the brink, I ran back to the sliver-bridge and cautiously studied it. Crevasses caused by strains from variations of the rate of motion of different parts of the glacier and by convexities in the channel are mere cracks when they first open,—so narrow as hardly to admit the blade of a pocket-knife,—and widen gradually, according to the extent of the strain. Now some of these cracks are interrupted like the cracks in wood, and, in opening, the strip of ice between overlapping ends is dragged out; and if the flow of the glacier there is such that no strain is made on the sliver, it maintains a continuous connection between the sides, just as the two sides of a slivered crack in wood that is being split are connected. Some crevasses remain open for years, and by the melting of their sides continue to increase in width long after the opening strain has ceased, while the sliver-bridges, level on top at first, and perfectly safe, are at length melted to thin, knife-edged blades, the upper portion being most exposed to the weather; and since the exposure is greatest in the middle, they at length curve downward like the cables of suspension-bridges. This one was evidently very old, for it had been wasted until it was the worst bridge I ever saw. The width of the crevasse was here about fifty feet, and the sliver, crossing diagonally, was about seventy feet long, was depressed twenty-five or thirty feet in the middle, and the up-curving ends were attached to the sides eight or ten feet below the surface of the glacier. Getting down the nearly vertical wall to the end of it and up the other side were the main difficulties, and they seemed all but insurmountable. Of the many perils encountered in my years of wandering in mountain altitudes, none seemed so plain and stern and merciless as this. And it was presented when we were wet to the skin and hungry, the sky was dark with snow, and the night near, and we had to fear the snow in our eyes and the disturbing action of the wind in any movement we might make. But we were forced to face it. It was a tremendous necessity.

Beginning not immediately above the sunken end of the bridge, but a little to one side, I cut nice hollows on the brink for my knees to rest in; then, leaning over, with my short-handled ax cut a step sixteen or eighteen inches below, which, on account of the sheerness of the wall, was shallow. That step, however, was well made; its floor sloped slightly inward, and formed a good hold for my heels. Then, slipping cautiously upon it, and crouching as low as possible, with my left side twisted toward the wall, I steadied myself with my left hand in a slight notch, while with the right I cut other steps and notches in succession, guarding against glinting of the ax, for life or death was in every stroke, and in the niceness of finish of every foothold. After the end of the bridge was reached, it was a delicate thing to poise on a little platform which I had chipped on its up-curving end, and, bending over the slippery surface, get astride of it. Crossing was easy, cutting off the sharp edge with careful strokes, and hitching forward a few inches at a time, keeping my balance with my knees pressed against its sides. The tremendous abyss on each side I studiously ignored. The surface of that blue sliver was then all the world. But the most trying part of the adventure was, after working my way across inch by inch, to rise from the safe position astride that slippery strip of ice, and to cut a ladder in the face of the wall—chipping, climbing, holding on with feet and fingers in mere notches. At such times one's whole body is eye, and common skill and fortitude are replaced by power beyond our call or knowledge. Never before had I been so long under deadly strain. How I got up the cliff at the end of the bridge I never could tell. The thing seemed to have been done by somebody else. I never have had contempt of death, though in the course of my explorations I oftentimes felt that to meet one's fate on a mountain, in a grand cañon, or in the heart of a crystal glacier would be blessed as compared with death from disease, a mean accident in a street, or from a sniff of sewer-gas. But the sweetest, cleanest death, set thus calmly and glaringly clear before us, is hard enough to face, even though we feel gratefully sure that we have already had happiness enough for a dozen lives.

But poor Stickeen, the wee, silky, sleekit beastie—think of him! When I had decided to try the bridge, and while I was on my knees cutting away the rounded brow, he came behind me, pushed his head past my shoulder, looked down and across, scanned the sliver and its approaches with his queer eyes, then looked me in the face with a startled air of surprise and concern, and began to mutter and whine, saying as plainly as if speaking with words, "Surely you are not going to try that awful place?" This was the first time I had seen him gaze deliberately into a crevasse or into my face with a speaking look. That he should have recognized and appreciated the danger at the first glance showed wonderful sagacity. Never before had the quick, daring midget seemed to know that ice was slippery, or that there was such a thing as danger anywhere. His looks and the tones of his voice when he began to complain and speak his fears were so human that I unconsciously talked to him as I would to a boy, and in trying to calm his fears perhaps in some measure moderated my own. "Hush your fears, my boy," I said; "we will get across safe, though it is not going to be easy. No right way is easy in this rough world. We must risk our lives to save them. At the worst we can only slip; and then how grand a grave we shall have! And by and by our nice bones will do good in the terminal moraine." But my sermon was far from reassuring him; he began to cry, and after taking another piercing look at the tremendous gulf, ran away in desperate excitement, seeking some other crossing. By the time he got back, baffled, of course, I had made a step or two. I dared not look back, but he made himself heard; and when he saw that I was certainly crossing, he cried aloud in despair. The danger was enough to daunt anybody, but it seems wonderful that he should have been able to weigh and appreciate it so justly. No mountaineer could have seen it more quickly or judged it more wisely, discriminating between real and apparent peril.

After I had gained the other side he howled louder than ever, and after running back and forth in vain search for a way of escape, he would return to the brink of the crevasse above the bridge, moaning and groaning as if in the bitterness of death. Could this be the silent, philosophic Stickeen? I shouted encouragement, telling him the bridge was not so bad as it looked, that I had left it flat for his feet, and he could walk it easily. But he was afraid to try it. Strange that so small an animal should be capable of such big, wise fears! I called again and again in a reassuring tone to come on and fear nothing; that he could come if he would only try. Then he would hush for a moment, look again at the bridge, and shout his unshakable conviction that he could never, never come that way; then lie back in despair, as if howling: "Oh-o-o, what a place! No-o-o; I can never go-o-o down there!" His natural composure and courage had vanished utterly in a tumultuous storm of fear. Had the danger been less, his distress would have seemed ridiculous. But in this gulf—a huge, yawning sepulcher big enough to hold everybody in the territory—lay the shadow of death, and his heartrending cries might well have called Heaven to his help. Perhaps they did. So hidden before, he was transparent now, and one could see the workings of his mind like the movements of a clock out of its case. His voice and gestures were perfectly human, and his hopes and fears unmistakable, while he seemed to understand every word of mine. I was troubled at the thought of leaving him. It seemed impossible to get him to venture. To compel him to try by fear of being left, I started off as if leaving him to his fate, and disappeared back of a hummock; but this did no good, for he only lay down and cried. So after hiding a few minutes, I went back to the brink of the crevasse, and in a severe tone of voice shouted across to him that now I must certainly leave him—I could wait no longer; and that if he would not come, all I could promise was that I would return to seek him next day. I warned him that if he went back to the woods the wolves would kill him, and finished by urging him once more by words and gestures to come on. He knew very well what I meant, and at last, with the courage of despair, hushed and breathless, he lay down on the brink in the hollow I had made for my knees, pressed his body against the ice to get the advantage of the friction, gazed into the first step, put his little feet together, and slid them slowly down into it, bunching all four in it, and almost standing on his head. Then, without lifting them, as well as I could see through the snow, he slowly worked them over the edge of the step, and down into the next and the next in succession in the same way, and gained the bridge. Then lifting his feet with the regularity and slowness of the vibrations of a seconds' pendulum, as if counting and measuring one, two, three, holding himself in dainty poise, and giving separate attention to each little step, he gained the foot of the cliff, at the top of which I was kneeling to give him a lift should he get within reach. Here he halted in dead silence, and it was here I feared he might fail, for dogs are poor climbers. I had no cord. If I had had one, I would have dropped a noose over his head and hauled him up. But while I was thinking whether an available cord might be made out of clothing, he was looking keenly into the series of notched steps and finger-holds of the ice-ladder I had made, as if counting them and fixing the position of each one in his mind. Then suddenly up he came, with a nervy, springy rush, hooking his paws into the notches and steps so quickly that I could not see how it was done, and whizzed past my head, safe at last!

And now came a scene! "Well done, well done, little boy! Brave boy!" I cried, trying to catch and caress him; but he would not be caught. Never before or since have I seen anything like so passionate a revulsion from the depths of despair to uncontrollable, exultant, triumphant joy. He flashed and darted hither and thither as if fairly demented, screaming and shouting, swirling round and round in giddy loops and circles like a leaf in a whirlwind, lying down and rolling over and over, sidewise and heels over head, pouring forth a tumultuous flood of hysterical cries and sobs and gasping mutterings. And when I ran up to him to shake him, fearing he might die of joy, he flashed off two or three hundred yards, his feet in a mist of motion; then, turning suddenly, he came back in wild rushes, and launched himself at my face, almost knocking me down, all the time screeching and screaming and shouting as if saying, "Saved! saved! saved!" Then away again, dropping suddenly at times with his feet in the air, trembling, and fairly sobbing. Such passionate emotion was enough to kill him. Moses's stately song of triumph after escaping the Egyptians and the Red Sea was nothing to it. Who could have guessed the capacity of the dull, enduring little fellow for all that most stirs this mortal frame? Nobody could have helped crying with him.

But there is nothing like work for toning down either excessive fear or joy. So I ran ahead, calling him, in as gruff a voice as I could command, to come on and stop his nonsense, for we had far to go, and it would soon be dark. Neither of us feared another trial like this. Heaven would surely count one enough for a lifetime. The ice ahead was gashed by thousands of crevasses, but they were common ones. The joy of deliverance burned in us like fire, and we ran without fatigue, every muscle, with immense rebound, glorying in its strength. Stickeen flew across everything in his way, and not till dark did he settle into his normal fox-like, gliding trot. At last the mountains crowned with spruce came in sight, looming faintly in the gloaming, and we soon felt the solid rock beneath our feet, and were safe. Then came weariness. We stumbled down along the lateral moraine in the dark, over rocks and tree-trunks, through the bushes and devil-club thickets and mossy logs and boulders of the woods where we had sheltered ourselves in the morning. Then out on the level mud-slope of the terminal moraine. Danger had vanished, and so had our strength. We reached camp about ten o'clock, and found a big fire and a big supper. A party of Hoona Indians had visited Mr. Young, bringing a gift of porpoise-meat and wild strawberries, and hunter Joe had brought in a wild goat. But we lay down, too tired to eat much, and soon fell into a troubled sleep. The man who said, "The harder the toil the sweeter the rest," never was profoundly tired. Stickeen kept springing up and muttering in his sleep, no doubt dreaming that he was still on the brink of the crevasse; and so did I— that night and many others, long afterward, when I was nervous and overtired.

Thereafter Stickeen was a changed dog. During the rest of the trip, instead of holding aloof, he would come to me at night, when all was quiet about the camp-fire, and rest his head on my knee, with a look of devotion, as if I were his god. And often, as he caught my eye, he seemed to be trying to say, "Wasn't that an awful time we had together on the glacier?"

None of his old friends know what finally became of him. When my work for the season was done I departed for California, and never saw the dear little fellow again. Mr. Young wrote me that in the summer of 1883 he was stolen by a tourist at Fort Wrangel, and taken away on a steamer. His fate is wrapped in mystery. If alive he is very old. Most likely he has left this world—crossed the last crevasse—and gone to another. But he will not be forgotten. Come what may, to me Stickeen is immortal.

JAMES STREET

Weep No More, My Lady

The moonlight symphony of swamp creatures hushed abruptly, and the dismal bog was as peaceful as unborn time and seemed to brood in its silence. The gaunt man glanced back at the boy and motioned for him to be quiet, but it was too late. Their presence was discovered. A jumbo frog rumbled a warning and the swamp squirmed into life as its denizens scuttled to safety.

Fox fire was glowing to the west and the bayou was slapping the cypress knees when suddenly a haunting laugh echoed through the wilderness, a strange chuckling yodel ending in a weird "gro-o-o."

The boy's eyes were wide and staring. "That's it, Uncle Jess. Come on! Let's catch it!"

"Uh, oh." The man gripped his shotgun. "That ain't no animal. That's a thing."

They hurried noiselessly in the direction of the sound that Skeeter had been hearing for several nights. Swamp born and reared, they feared nothing they could shoot or outwit, so they slipped out of the morass and to the side of a ridge. Suddenly, Jesse put out his hand and stopped the child, then pointed up the slope. The animal, clearly visible in the moonlight, was sitting on its haunches, its head cocked sideways as it chuckled. It was a merry and rather melodious little chuckle.

Skeeter grinned in spite of his surprise, then said, "Sh-h-h. It'll smell us."

Jesse said, "Can't nothing smell that far. Wonder what the durn thing is?" He peered up the ridge, studying the creature. He had no intention of shooting unless attacked, for Jesse Tolliver and his nephew never killed wantonly.

The animal, however, did smell them and whipped her nose into the wind, crouched and braced. She was about sixteen inches high and weighed twenty-two pounds. Her coat was red and silky and there was a blaze of white down her chest and a circle of white around her throat. Her face was wrinkled and sad, like a wise old man's.

Jesse shook his head. "Looks som'n like a mixture of bloodhound and terrier from here," he whispered. "It beats me—"

"It's a dog, all right," Skeeter said.

"Can't no dog laugh."

"That dog can." The boy began walking toward the animal, his right hand outstretched. "Heah. Heah. I ain't gonna hurt you."

The dog, for she was a dog, cocked her head from one side to the other and watched Skeeter. She was trembling, but she didn't run. And when Skeeter knelt by her, she stopped trembling, for the ways of a boy with a dog are mysterious. He stroked her, and the trim little creature looked up at him and blinked her big hazel eyes. Then she turned over and Skeeter scratched her. She closed her eyes, stretched and chuckled, a happy mixture of chortle and yodel. Jesse ambled up and the dog leaped to her feet and sprang between the boy and the man.

Skeeter calmed her. "That's just Uncle Jess."

Jesse, still bewildered, shook his head again. "I still say that ain't no dog. She don't smell and she don't bark. Ain't natural. And look at her! Licking herself like a cat."

"Well, I'll be a catty wampus," Skeeter said. "Never saw a dog do that before." However, he was quick to defend any mannerism of his friend and said, "She likes to keep herself clean. She's a lady and I'm gonna name her that, and she's mine 'cause I found her."

"Lady, huh?"

"No, sir. My Lady. If I name her just plain Lady, how folks gonna know she's mine?" He began stroking his dog again. "Gee m'netty, Uncle Jess, I ain't never had nothing like this before."

"It still don't make sense to me," Jesse said. But he didn't care, for he was happy because the child was happy.

Like most mysteries, there was no mystery at all about My Lady. She was a lady, all right, an aristocratic Basenji, one of those strange barkless dogs of Africa. Her ancestors were pets of the Pharaohs and her line was well established when the now proud races of men were wandering about Europe, begging handouts from Nature. A bundle of nerves and muscles, she would fight anything, and could scent game up to eighty yards. She had the gait of an antelope and was odorless, washing herself before and after meals. However, the only noises she could make were a piercing cry that sounded almost human and that chuckling little chortle. She could chuckle only when happy and she had been happy in the woods. Now she was happy again.

As most men judge values, she was worth more than all the possessions of Jesse and his nephew. Several of the dogs had been shipped to New Orleans to avoid the dangerous upper route, thence by motor to a Northern kennel. While crossing Mississippi, My Lady had escaped from the station wagon. Her keeper had advertised in several papers, but Jesse and Skeeter never saw papers.

Skeeter said, "Come on, M'Lady. Let's go home."

The dog didn't hesitate, but walked proudly at the boy's side to a cabin on the bank of the bayou. Skeeter crumbled corn bread, wet it with pot likker and put it before her. She sniffed the food disdainfully at first, then ate it only when she saw the boy fix a bowl for his uncle. She licked herself clean and explored the cabin, sniffing the brush brooms, the piles of wild pecans and hickory nuts, and then the cots. Satisfied at last, she jumped on Skeeter's bed, tucked her nose under her paws and went to sleep.

"Acts like she owns the place," Jesse said.

"Where you reckon she came from?" The boy slipped his overall straps from his shoulders, flexed his stringy muscles and yawned.

"Lord knows. Circus maybe." He looked at M'Lady quickly. "Say, maybe she's a freak and run off from some show. Bet they'd give us two dollars for her."

Skeeter's face got long. "You don't aim to get rid of her?"

The old man put his shotgun over the mantel and lit his pipe. "Skeets, if you want that thing, I wouldn't get shed of her for a piece of bottom land a mile long. Already plowed and planted."

"I reckoned you wouldn't."

Jesse sat down and leaned back, blowing smoke into the air to drive away mosquitoes. The boy got a brick and hammer and began cracking nuts, pounding the meat to pulp so his uncle could chew it. Skeeter's yellow hair hadn't been cut for months and was tangled. He had freckles too. And his real name was Jonathan. His mother was Jesse's only sister and died when the child was born. No one thereabouts ever knew what happened to his father. Jesse, a leathery, toothless old man with faded blue eyes, took him to bring up and called him Skeeter because he was so little.

In the village, where Jesse seldom visited, folks wondered

if he were fit'n to rear a little boy. They considered him shiftless and no-count. Jesse had lived all of his sixty years in the swamp and his way of life was a torment to folks who believed life must be lived by rules. He earned a few dollars selling jumbo frogs and pelts, but mostly he just paddled around the swamp, watching things and teaching Skeeter about life.

The villagers might have tried to send Skeeter to an orphanage, but for Joe (Cash) Watson, the storekeeper. Cash was a hard man, but fair. He often hunted with Jesse, and the old man had trained Cash's dogs. When there was talk of sending Skeeter away, Cash said, "You ain't agonna do it. You just don't take young'uns away from their folks." And that's all there was to it.

Jesse never coveted the "frills and furbelows of damnfool folks" and yearned for only two things—a twenty-gauge shotgun for Skeeter and a set of Roebuckers for himself, as he called store-bought teeth. Cash had promised him the gun and the best false teeth in the catalogue for forty-six dollars. Jesse had saved $9.37.

"Someday I'm gonna get them Roebuckers," he often told Skeeter. "Then I'm gonna eat me enough roastin' ears to kill a goat. Maybe I can get a set with a couple of gold teeth in 'em. I seen a man one time with six gold teeth."

Once Skeeter asked him, "Why don't you get a job with the W. P. and A. and make enough money to buy them Roebuckers?"

"I don't want 'em that bad," Jesse said.

So he was happy for Skeeter to have M'Lady, thinking the dog would sort of make up for the shotgun.

The boy cracked as many nuts as his uncle wanted, then put the hammer away. He was undressing when he glanced over at his dog. "Gosh, Uncle Jess. I'm scared somebody'll come get her."

"I ain't heard of nobody losing no things around here. If'n

they had, they'd been to me 'fo' now, being's I know all about dogs and the swamp."

"That's so," Skeeter said. "But you don't reckon she belonged to another fellow like me, do you? I know how I'd feel if I had a dog like her and she got lost."

Jesse said, "She didn't belong to another fellow like you. If'n she had, she wouldn't be so happy here."

Skeeter fed M'Lady biscuits and molasses for breakfast, and although the Basenji ate it, she still was hungry when she went into the swamp with the boy. He was hoping he could find a bee tree or signs of wild hogs. They were at the edge of a clearing when M'Lady's chokebore nose suddenly tilted and she froze to a flash point, pausing only long enough to get set. Then she darted to the bayou, at least sixty yards away, dived into a clump of reeds and snatched a water rat. She was eating it when Skeeter ran up.

"Don't do that," he scolded. "Ain't you got no more sense than run into water after things? A snake or a gator might snatch you."

The Basenji dropped the rat and tucked her head. She knew the boy was displeased, and when she looked up at him her eyes were filled and a woe-begone expression was on her face.

Skeeter tried to explain, "I didn't mean to hurt your feelings. Don't cry." He stepped back quickly and stared at her, at the tears in her eyes. "She *is* crying! Be John Brown!" Skeeter called her and ran toward the cabin, where Jesse was cutting splinters.

"Uncle Jess! Guess what else my dog can do!"

"Whistle?" the old man laughed.

"She can cry! I declare to goodness! Not out loud, but she can cry just the same."

Jesse knew that most dogs will get watery-eyed on occasion, but, not wanting to ridicule M'Lady's accomplishments, asked, "What made her cry?"

"Well, sir, we were walking along and all of a sudden she got a scent and flash pointed and then—" Skeeter remembered something.

"Then what?"

Skeeter sat on the steps. "Uncle Jess," he said slowly, "we must have been fifty or sixty yards from that rat when she smelled it."

"What rat? What's eating you?"

The child told him the story and Jesse couldn't believe it. For a dog to pick up the scent of a water rat at sixty yards simply isn't credible. Jesse reckoned Skeeter's love for M'Lady had led him to exaggerate.

Skeeter knew Jesse didn't believe the story, so he said, "Come on. I'll show you." He whistled for M'Lady.

The dog came up. "Hey," Jesse said. "That thing knows what a whistle means. Shows she's been around folks." He caught the dog's eye and commanded, "Heel!"

But M'Lady cocked her head quizzically. Then she turned to the boy and chuckled softly. She'd never heard the order before. That was obvious. Her nose came up into the breeze and she wheeled.

Her curved tail suddenly was still and her head was poised.

"Flash pointing," Jesse said. "Well, I'll be a monkey's uncle!"

M'Lady held the strange point only for a second, though, then dashed toward a corn patch about eighty yards from the cabin.

Halfway to the patch, she broke her gait and began creeping. A whir of feathered lightning sounded in the corn and a covey of quail exploded almost under her nose. She sprang and snatched a bird.

"Partridges!" Jesse's jaw dropped.

The child was as motionless as stone, his face white and his eyes wide in amazement. Finally he found his voice, "She was right here when she smelled them birds. A good eighty yards."

"I know she ain't no dog now," Jesse said. "Can't no dog do that."

"She's fast as greased lightning and ain't scared of nothing." Skeeter still was under the spell of the adventure. "She's a hunting dog from way back."

"She ain't no dog a-tall, I'm telling you. It ain't human." Jesse walked toward M'Lady and told her to fetch the bird, but the dog didn't understand. Instead, she pawed it. "Well," Jesse said. "One thing's certain. She ain't no bird hunter."

"She can do anything," Skeeter said. "Even hunt birds. Maybe I can make a bird dog out'n her. Wouldn't that be som'n?"

"You're batty. Maybe a coon dog, but not a bird dog. I know 'bout dogs."

"Me too," said Skeeter. And he did. He'd seen Jesse train many dogs, even pointers, and had helped him train Big Boy, Cash Watson's prize gun dog.

Jesse eyed Skeeter and read his mind.

"It can't be done, Skeets."

"Maybe not, but I aim to try. Any dog can run coons and rabbits, but it takes a pure D humdinger to hunt birds. Ain't no sin in trying, is it?"

"Naw," Jesse said slowly. "But she'll flush birds."

"I'll learn her not to."

"She won't hold no point. Any dog'll flash point. And she'll hunt rats."

"I'm gonna learn her just to hunt birds. And I'm starting right now," Skeeter said. He started walking away, then turned. "I seen a man once train a razorback hawg to point birds. You know as good as me that if a dog's got pure D hoss sense and a fellow's got bat brains, he can train the dog to hunt birds."

"Wanta bet?" Jesse issued the challenge in an effort to keep Skeeter's enthusiasm and determination at the high-water mark.

"Yes, sir. If I don't train my dog, then I'll cut all the splinters for a year. If I do, you cut 'em."

"It's a go," Jesse said.

Skeeter ran to the bayou and recovered the rat M'Lady had killed. He tied it around his dog's neck. The Basenji was indignant and tried to claw off the hateful burden. Failing, she ran into the house and under a bed, but Skeeter made her come out. M'Lady filled up then and her face assumed that nobody-loves-me look. The boy steeled himself, tapped M'Lady's nose with the rat, and left it around her neck.

"You done whittled out a job for yourself," Jesse said. "If'n you get her trained, you'll lose her in the brush. She's too fast and too little to keep up with."

"I'll bell her," Skeeter said. "I'm gonna learn her ever'thing. I got us a gun dog, Uncle Jess."

The old man sat on the porch and propped against the wall. "Bud, I don't know what that thing is. But you're a thoroughbred. John dog my hide!"

If Skeeter had loved M'Lady one bit less, his patience would have exploded during the ordeal of training the Basenji. It takes judgment and infinite patience to train a bird dog properly, but to train a Basenji, that'll hunt anything, to concentrate only on quail took something more than discipline and patience. It never could have been done except for that strange affinity between a boy and a dog.

M'Lady's devotion to Skeeter was so complete that she was anxious to do anything to earn a pat. It wasn't difficult to teach her to heel and follow at Skeeter's feet regardless of the urge to dash away and chase rabbits. The boy used a clothesline as a guide rope and made M'Lady follow him. The first time the dog tried to chase an animal, Skeeter pinched the rope around her neck just a bit and commanded, "Heel!" And when she obeyed, Skeeter released the noose. It took

M'Lady only a few hours to associate disobedience with disfavor.

The dog learned that when she chased and killed a rat or rabbit, the thing would be tied around her neck. The only things she could hunt without being disciplined were quail. Of course, she often mistook the scent of game chickens for quails and hunted them, but Skeeter punished her by scolding. He never switched his dog, but to M'Lady a harsh word from the boy hurt more than a hickory limb.

Jesse watched the dog's progress and pretended not to be impressed. He never volunteered suggestions. M'Lady learned quickly, but the task of teaching her to point birds seemed hopeless. Skeets knew she'd never point as pointers do, so he worked out his own system. He taught her to stand motionless when he shouted "Hup!" One day she got a scent of birds, paused or pointed for a moment as most animals will, and was ready to spring away when Skeeter said "Hup!"

M'Lady was confused. Every instinct urged her to chase the birds, but her master had said stand still. She broke, however, and Skeeter scolded her. She pouted at first, then filled up, but the boy ignored her until she obeyed the next command, then he patted her and she chuckled.

The lessons continued for days and weeks, and slowly and surely M'Lady learned her chores. She learned that the second she smelled birds she must stop and stand still until Skeeter flushed them. That she must not quiver when he shot.

Teaching her to fetch was easy, but teaching her to retrieve dead birds without damaging them was another matter. M'Lady had a hard mouth—that is, she sank her teeth into the birds. Skeeter used one of the oldest hunting tricks of the backwoods to break her.

He got a stick and wrapped it with wire and taught his dog to fetch it. Only once did M'Lady bite hard on the stick, and then the wire hurt her sensitive mouth. Soon she developed a habit of carrying the stick on her tongue and supporting it lightly with her teeth. Skeeter tied quail feathers on the stick, and soon M'Lady's education was complete.

Skeeter led Jesse into a field one day and turned his dog loose. She flashed to a point almost immediately. It was a funny point and Jesse almost laughed. The dog's curved tail poked up over her back, she spraddled her front legs and sort of squatted, her nose pointing the birds, more than forty yards away. She remained rigid until the boy flushed and shot, then she leaped away, seeking and fetching dead birds.

Jesse was mighty proud. "Well, Skeets, looks like you got yourself a bird hunter."

"Yes, sir," Skeeter said. "And you got yourself a job." He pointed toward the kindling pile.

The swamp was dressing for winter when Cash Watson drove down that day to give his Big Boy a workout in the wild brush.

He fetched Jesse a couple of cans of smoking tobacco and Skeeter a bag of peppermint jawbreakers. He locked his fine pointer in the corncrib for the night and was warming himself in the cabin when he noticed M'Lady for the first time. She was sleeping in front of the fire.

"What's that?" he asked.

"My dog," said Skeeter. "Ain't she a beaut?"

"She sure is," Cash grinned at Jesse. Skeeter went out to the well and Cash asked his old friend, "What the devil kind of mutt is that?"

"Search me," Jesse said. "Skeets found her in the swamp. I reckon she's got a trace of bloodhound in her and some terrier and a heap of just plain dog."

M'Lady cocked one ear and got up and stretched; then, apparently not liking the company, turned her tail toward Cash and strutted out, looking for Skeeter.

The men laughed. "Som'n wrong with her throat," Jesse

said. "She can't bark. When she tries, she makes a funny sound, sort of a cackling, chuckling yodel. Sounds like she's laughing."

"Well," Cash said, "trust a young'un to love the orner'st dog he can find."

"Wait a minute," Jesse said. "She ain't no-count. She's a bird-hunting fool."

Just then Skeeter entered and Cash jestingly said, "Hear you got yourself a bird dog, son."

The boy clasped his hands behind him and rocked on the balls of his feet as he had seen the men do. "Well, now, I'll tell you, Mr. Cash. M'Lady does ever'thing except tote the gun."

"She must be fair to middling. Why not take her out with Big Boy tomorrow? Do my dog good to hunt in a brace."

"Me and my dog don't want to show Big Boy up. He's a pretty good ol' dog."

"Whoa!" Cash was every inch a bird-dog man and nobody could challenge him without a showdown. Besides, Skeeter was shooting up and should be learning a few things about life. "Any old boiler can pop off steam." Cash winked at Jesse.

"Well, now, sir, if you're itching for a run, I'll just double-dog dare you to run your dog against mine. And anybody who'll take a dare will pull up young cotton and push a widow woman's ducks in the water."

Cash admired the boy's confidence. "All right, son. It's a deal. What are the stakes?"

Skeeter started to mention the twenty-gauge gun he wanted, but changed his mind quickly. He reached down and patted M'Lady, then looked up. "If my dog beats yours, then you get them Roebuckers for Uncle Jess."

Jesse's chest suddenly was tight. Cash glanced from the boy to the man and he, too, was proud of Skeeter. "I wasn't aiming to go that high. But all right. What do I get if I win?"

"I'll cut you ten cords of stovewood."

"And a stack of splinters?"

"Yes, sir."

Cash offered his hand and Skeeter took it. "It's a race," Cash said. "Jesse will be the judge."

The wind was rustling the sage and there was a nip in the early-morning air when they took the dogs to a clearing and set them down. Skeeter snapped a bell around M'Lady's neck and, at word from Jesse, the dogs were released.

Big Boy bounded away and began circling, ranging into the brush. M'Lady tilted her nose into the wind and ripped away toward the sage, her bell tinkling. Cash said, "She sure covers ground." Skeeter made no effort to keep up with her, but waited until he couldn't hear the bell, then ran for a clearing where he had last heard it. And there was M'Lady on a point.

Cash almost laughed out loud. "That ain't no point, son. That's a squat."

"She's got birds."

"Where?"

Jesse leaned against a tree and watched the fun.

Skeeter pointed toward a clump of sage. "She's pointing birds in that sage."

Cash couldn't restrain his mirth. "Boy, now that's what I call some pointing. Why, Skeeter, it's sixty or seventy yards to that sage."

Just then Big Boy flashed by M'Lady, his head high. He raced to the edge of the sage, caught the wind, then whipped around, freezing to a point. Cash called Jesse's attention to the point.

"That's M'Lady's point," Skeeter said. "She's got the same birds Big Boy has."

Jesse sauntered up. "The boy's right, Cash. I aimed to keep my mouth out'n this race, but M'Lady is pointing them birds. She can catch scents up to eighty yards."

Cash said, "Aw, go on. You're crazy." He walked over and flushed the birds.

Skeeter picked one off and ordered M'Lady to fetch. When she returned with the bird, the boy patted her and she began chuckling.

Cash really studied her then for the first time. "Hey!" he said suddenly. "A Basenji! That's a Basenji!"

"A what?" Jesse asked.

"I should have known." Cash was very excited. "That's the dog that was lost by them rich Yankees. I saw about it in the paper." He happened to look at Skeeter then and wished he had cut out his tongue.

The boy's lips were compressed and his face was drawn and white. Jesse had closed his eyes and was rubbing his forehead.

Cash, trying to dismiss the subject, said, "Just 'cause it was in the paper don't make it so. I don't believe that's the same dog, come to think of it."

"Do you aim to tell 'em where the dog is?" Skeeter asked.

Cash looked at Jesse, then at the ground. "It ain't none of my business."

"How 'bout you, Uncle Jess?"

"I ain't telling nobody nothin'."

"I know she's the same dog," Skeeter said. "On account of I just know it. But she's mine now." His voice rose and trembled. "And ain't nobody gonna take her away from me." He ran into the swamp. M'Lady was at his heels.

Cash said, "Durn my lip. I'm sorry, Jesse. If I'd kept my big mouth shut he'd never known the difference."

"It can't be helped now," Jesse said.

" 'Course she beat Big Boy. Them's the best hunting dogs in the world. And she's worth a mint of money."

They didn't feel up to hunting and returned to the cabin and sat on the porch. Neither had much to say, but kept

"That's no point, son. That's a squat."

glancing toward the swamp where Skeeter and M'Lady were walking along the bayou. "Don't you worry," he said tenderly. "Ain't nobody gonna bother you."

He sat on a stump and M'Lady put her head on his knee. She wasn't worrying. Nothing could have been more contented than she was.

"I don't care if the sheriff comes down." Skeeter pulled her onto his lap and held her. "I don't give a whoop if the governor comes down. Even the president of the United States! The whole shebang can come, but ain't nobody gonna mess with you."

His words gave him courage and he felt better, but for only a minute. Then the tug-of-war between him and his conscience started.

"Once I found a Barlow knife and kept it and it was all right," he mumbled.

But this is different.

"Finders, keepers; losers, weepers."

No, Skeeter.

"Well, I don't care. She's mine."

Remember what your Uncle Jess said.

"He said a heap of things."

Yes, but you remember one thing more than the rest. He said, "Certain things are right and certain things are wrong. And nothing ain't gonna ever change that. When you learn that, then you're fit'n to be a man." Remember, Skeeter?

A feeling of despair and loneliness almost overwhelmed him. He fought off the tears as long as he could, but finally he gave in, and his sobs caused M'Lady to peer into his face and wonder why he was acting that way when she was so happy. He put his arms around her neck and pulled her to him. "My li'l old puppy dog. Poor li'l old puppy dog."

He sniffed back his tears and got up and walked to the cabin. M'Lady curled up by the fire and the boy sat down, watching the logs splutter for several minutes. Then he said, almost in a whisper, "Uncle Jess, if you keep som'n that ain't yours, it's the same as stealing, ain't it?"

Cash leaned against the mantel and stared into the fire.

Jesse puffed his pipe slowly. "Son, that's som'n you got to settle with yourself."

Skeeter stood and turned his back to the flames, warming his hands. "Mr. Cash," he said slowly, "When you get back to your store, please let them folks know their dog is here."

"If that's how it is—"

"That's how it is," Skeeter said.

The firelight dancing on Jesse's face revealed the old man's dejection, and Skeeter, seeing it, said quickly, "It's best for M'Lady. She's too good for the swamp. They'll give her a good home."

Jesse flinched, and Cash, catching the hurt look in his friend's eyes, said, "Your dog outhunted mine, Skeets. You win them Roebuckers for your uncle."

"I don't want 'em," Jesse said, rather childishly. "I don't care if'n I never eat no roastin' ears." He got up quickly and hurried outside. Cash reckoned he'd better be going, and left Skeeter by the fire, rubbing his dog.

Jesse came back in directly and pulled up a chair. Skeeter started to speak, but Jesse spoke first. "I been doing a heap of thinking lately. You're sprouting up. The swamp ain't no place for you."

Skeets forgot about his dog and faced his uncle, bewildered.

"I reckon you're too good for the swamp, too," Jesse said. "I'm aiming to send you into town for a spell. I can make enough to keep you in fit'n clothes and all." He dared not look at the boy.

"Uncle Jess!" Skeets said reproachfully. "You don't mean that. You're just saying that on account of what I said about M'Lady. I said it just to keep you from feeling so bad about our dog going away. Gee m'netty, Uncle Jess. I ain't ever gonna leave you." He buried his face in his uncle's shoulder. M'Lady put her head on Jesse's knee and he patted the boy and rubbed the dog.

"Reckon I'll take them Roebuckers," he said at last. "I been wanting some for a long, long time."

Several days later Cash drove down and told them the man from the kennels was at his store. Skeeter didn't say a word, but called M'Lady and they got in Cash's car. All the way to town, the boy was silent. He held his dog's head in his lap.

The keeper took just one look at M'Lady and said, "That's she, all right. Miss Congo III." He turned to speak to Skeeter, but the boy was walking away. He got a glance at Skeeter's face, however. "Hell," he muttered. "I wish you fellows hadn't told me. I hate to take a dog away from a kid."

"He wanted you to know," Cash said.

"Mister"—Jesse closed his left eye and struck his swapping pose—"I'd like to swap you out'n that hound. Now, course she ain't much 'count—"

The keeper smiled in spite of himself. "If she was mine, I'd give her to the kid. But she's not for sale. The owner wants to breed her and establish her line in this country. And if she was for sale, she'd cost more money than any of us will ever see." He called Skeets and offered his hand. Skeets shook it.

"You're a good kid. There's a reward for this dog."

"I don't want no reward." The boy's words tumbled out. "I don't want nothing, except to be left alone. You've got your dog, mister. Take her and go on. Please." He walked away again, fearing he would cry.

Cash said, "I'll take the reward and keep it for him. Some-day he'll want it."

Jesse went out to the store porch to be with Skeeter. The keeper handed Cash the money. "It's tough, but the kid'll get over it. The dog never will."

"Is that a fact?"

"Yep. I know the breed. They never forget. That dog'll never laugh again. They never laugh unless they're happy."

He walked to the post where Skeeter had tied M'Lady. He untied the leash and started toward his station wagon. M'Lady braced her front feet and looked around for the boy. Seeing him on the porch, she jerked away from the keeper and ran to her master.

She rubbed against his legs. Skeets tried to ignore her. The keeper reached for the leash again and M'Lady crouched, baring her fangs. The keeper shrugged, a helpless gesture.

"Wild elephants couldn't pull that dog away from that boy," he said.

"That's all right, mister." Skeets unsnapped the leash and tossed it to the keeper. Then he walked to the station wagon, opened the door of a cage and called, "Heah, M'Lady!" She bounded to him. "Up!" he commanded. She didn't hesitate, but leaped into the cage. The keeper locked the door.

M'Lady, having obeyed a command, poked her nose between the bars, expecting a pat. The boy rubbed her head. She tried to move closer to him, but the bars held her. She looked quizzically at the bars, then tried to nudge them aside. Then she clawed them. A look of fear suddenly came to her eyes and she fastened them on Skeets, wistfully at first, then pleadingly. She couldn't make a sound, for her unhappiness had sealed her throat. Slowly her eyes filled up.

"Don't cry no more, M'Lady. Ever'thing's gonna be all right." He reached out to pat her, but the station wagon moved off, leaving him standing there in the dust.

Back on the porch, Jesse lit his pipe and said to his friend, "Cash, the boy has lost his dog and I've lost a boy."

"Aw, Jesse, Skeeter wouldn't leave you."

"That ain't what I mean. He's growed up, Cash. He don't look no older, but he is. He growed up that day in the swamp."

Skeeter walked into the store and Cash followed him. "I've got that reward for you, Jonathan."

It was the first time anyone ever had called him that and it sounded like man talk.

"And that twenty-gauge is waiting for you," Cash said. "I'm gonna give it to you."

"Thank you, Mr. Cash." The boy bit his lower lip. "But I don't aim to do no more hunting. I don't never want no more dogs."

"Know how you feel. But if you change your mind, the gun's here for you."

Skeets looked back toward the porch where Jesse was waiting, and said, "Tell you what, though. When you get them Roebuckers, get some with a couple of gold teeth in 'em. Take it out of the reward money."

"Sure, Jonathan."

Jesse joined them, and Skeeter said, "We better be getting back toward the house."

"I'll drive you down," Cash said. "But first I aim to treat you to some lemon pop and sardines."

"That's mighty nice of you," Jesse said, "but we better be gettin' on."

"What's the hurry?" Cash opened the pop.

"It's my time to cut splinters," Jesse said.

BEN AMES WILLIAMS

Mine Enemy's Dog

Fraternity has not changed in a hundred years; yet is there always some new thing in Fraternity. It may be only that Lee Motley's sow has killed her pigs, or that choleric Old Man Varney has larruped his thirty-year-old son with an ax helve, or that Jean Bubier has bought six yearling steers. But there is always some word of news, for the nightly interchange in Will Bissell's store, before the stage comes in with the mail. You may see the men gather there, a little after milking time, coming from the clean, white houses that are strung like beads along the five roads which lead into the village. A muscular, competent lot of men in their comfortable, homely garments. And they sit about the stove, and talk, and smoke, and spit, and laugh at the tales that are told.

Fraternity lies in a country of little towns and villages, with curious names something more than a century old. Liberty is west of Fraternity, Union is to the southward, Freedom and Equality lie north and west. Well enough named, these villages, too. Life in them flows easily; there is no great striving after more things than one man can use. The men are content to get their gardening quickly done so that they may trail the brooks for trout; they hurry with their winter's wood to find free time for woodcock and pa'tridge; and when the snow lies, they go into the woods with trap for mink or hound for fox.

Thirty years ago there were farms around Fraternity, and the land was clear; but young men have gone, and old men have died, and the birches and the alders and the pines have taken back the land. There are moose and deer in the swamps, and a wildcat or two, and up in Freedom a man killed a bear a year ago. . . .

The hills brood over these villages, blue and deeper blue from range to farther range. There is a bold loveliness about the land. The forests, blotched darkly with evergreens, or lightly splattered with the gay tops of the birches, clothe the ridges in garments of somber beauty. Toward sunset a man may stand upon these hilltops and look westward into the purple of the hills and the crimson of the sky until his eyes are drunk with looking. Or in the dark shadows down along the river he may listen to the trembling silences until he hears his pulses pound. And now and then, with a sense of unreality, you will come upon a deer along some old wood road; or a rabbit will fluster from some bush and rise on haunches, twenty yards away.

The talk in Will Bissell's store turns, night by night, upon these creatures of the woods that lie about the town; and by the same token the talk is filled with speech concerning dogs. The cult of the dog is strong in Fraternity. Every man has one dog, some have two. These, you will understand, are real dogs. No mongrels here; no sneaking, hungry, yapping curs. Predominant, the English setter, gentlest and kindest and best-natured of all breeds; and, in second place, the lop-eared hounds. A rabbit hound here and there; but not many of these. Foxhounds more often. Awkward, low-bodied, heavy dogs that will nevertheless nose out a fox and push him hard for mile on mile. These are not such foxhounds as run in packs for the sport of red-coated men. These are utilitarian dogs; their function is to keep the fox moving until the hunter can post himself for a shot. A fox skin is worth money; and cash money is scarce in Fraternity, as in all such little towns, and very hard to come by.

There are few sheep in Fraternity, so the dogs are free of that temptation; but there are deer. The deer is sacrosanct, to be taken only with rifle and ball, and by a woodcraft that bests the wild thing at its own game. No dog may justly chase a deer; and a dog so pursuing is outlawed and may legally be shot by any man. Men without conscience and dogs without honor will thus pursue the deer, in season and out; nevertheless, deer running is for the dogs of Fraternity the black and shameful crime.

They were talking dogs, on a certain night in late September, in Will Bissell's store. A dozen men were there; most of them from the village itself, two or three from outlying farms. Jim and Bert Saladine, both keen hunters of the deer, who killed their legal quota year by year, leaned side by side against the candy counter, and Andy Wattles sold them licorice sticks. Lee Motley had driven down from his farm above the Whitcher Swamp; and Jean Bubier had come in from the head of the Pond; and there was Gay Hunt; and there was George Freeland, and two or three besides. Proutt was one of these others, Proutt of South Fraternity, a farmer, a fox hunter, and a trainer of setter dogs. Finally, Nick Westley, a North Fraternity man, appointed within six months' time to be game warden for the district; a gentle man, well liked in spite of his thankless job; a man with a sense of humor, a steady and persistent courage, and a kindly tongue.

This night, as it happened, was to be the beginning of the enmity between Proutt and Westley. One-sided at first, this ill feeling. Two-sided at the last, and bitter enough on either side. A strange thing, dramatic enough in its development, fit to be numbered among the old men's tales that were told around the stove. . . .

Proutt, the dog trainer, was a man who knew dogs. None denied him that. "Yes," they would say; "Proutt'll break a dog for you. And when he gits done with your dog, your dog'll mind." If you scented some reservation in word or tone, and asked a question, you got no explanation. But your informant might say casually: "Hepperton's a good man with a dog, too. Over in Liberty. Gentles 'em."

Persistent inquiry might have brought out the fact that Hepperton never whipped a dog; that Proutt knew no other method. Lee Motley, who loved dogs, used to tell an incident. "Went out with Proutt once," he would explain. "After woodcock, we was. He was breaking a two-year-old. Nice a dog as I ever see. First bird, she took a nice point; but she broke shot. He had him a rawhide strap; and he called her in and I never see a dog hurt worse. And after that he couldn't get her out from under his legs. Ain't been out with him since. Not me."

Proutt was not liked. He was a morose man, and severe, and known to nurse a grudge. But he turned out dogs which knew their business, and none denied him this. So had he his measure of respect; and his neighbors minded their own affairs and kept out of the man's harsh path.

Curiously enough, though he trained setters, Proutt did not like them. He preferred the hound; and his own dog—a lop-eared brown-and-white named Dan—was his particular pride. This pride was like the pride of a new father; it showed itself in much talk of Dan's deeds and Dan's virtues, so that Fraternity's ears were wearied with the name of Dan, and it was the fashion to grin in one's sleeve at Proutt's tales and to discredit them.

Proutt spoke, this night, of a day's hunting of the winter before. How, coursing the woods, he had heard a hound's bay far below him, and had taken post upon a ledge across which he thought the fox would come. "Dan 'uz with me," he said, in his hoarse loud voice. "I says to Dan: 'Set,' and he set on his ha'nches, right aside me, cocking his nose down where t'other dog was baying, waiting, wise as an owl.

"I had my old gun, with Number Threes in both bar'ls; and me and Dan stayed there, awaiting; and the baying come nearer all the time, till I see the fox would come acrost that ledge, sure.

"Cold it was. Wind ablowing, and the snow acutting past my ears. Not much snow on the ground; but it was froze hard as sand. I figured Dan'd get uneasy; but he never stirred. Set where I'd told him to set; and us awaiting.

"Time come, I see the fox, sneaking up the ledge at that long, easy lope o' theirs. Dan see him too. His ears lifted and he looked my way. I says: 'Set.' And he let his ears down again, and stayed still. Fox come along, 'bout five rods below us. Crossed over there. So fur away I knowed I couldn't drop him. Never pulled; and he never saw me; and old Dan set where he was. Never moved a mite.

"After a spell, Will Belter's hound come past; and then come Will himself, cutting down from where he'd been waiting. Says: 'See a fox go by?' And I told him I did. He ast why I didn't shoot; and I says the fox was too fur off. And he says: 'Where was your dog?' So I told him Dan was setting right by me."

Proutt laughed harshly, and slapped a triumphant hand upon his knee. "Will wouldn't believe me," he declared, "till I showed him tracks, where we wuz, and where the fox went by."

He looked around for their admiration; but no one spoke at all. Only one or two glanced sidewise at each other, and slowly grinned. The tale was all right, except for a thing or two. In the first place, Proutt was no man to let a fox go by, no matter how long the shot; and, in the second place, Dan was known to be a surly dog, not overly obedient, unruly as his master. And, in the third place, this incident, thoroughly authenticated, had happened two years before to another man and another dog, as everyone in the store knew. Proutt had borrowed his tale from a source too close home. . . .

So they knew he lied; but no one cared to tell him so. Only, after a little silence, Nick Westley, the game warden, said with a slow twinkle in his eye: "Proutt, that reminds me of a story my father used to tell."

Proutt grunted something or other, disgusted with their lack of appreciation; and Westley took it for encouragement, and began to whittle slow, fine shavings from a sliver of pine which he held in hand, and told the tale.

"It was when he was younger," he explained, "before he was married, while he still lived at home. But I've heard him tell the story many a time.

"My Uncle Jim was living then; and he and my father had a hound. Good dog he was too. Good as Dan, I think, Proutt.

"Well, one winter morning, with six or eight inches of loose snow on the ground, they were working up some wood in the shed; and they saw the old hound drift off into the pasture and up the hill. And after a spell they heard him yelling down by the river.

"Jim said to my father: 'He's got a fox.' And father said: 'Jim, let's go get that fox.' So they dropped their axes, and went in and got their guns, and they worked up through the pasture and over the hill till they located the dog's noise, and they figured the fox would come up around the hill by a certain way; and so they posted themselves there, one on either side of the path they thought he would take. And set to waiting. And it was cold as could be, and cold waiting, and they stamped their feet a little, but they couldn't move much for fear the fox would see them.

"So they were both well pleased when they saw the fox coming; and they both shot when he came in range, because they were cold and in a hurry and anxious to be done.

"Well, they shot into each other. Jim yelled: 'Damn it, my legs are full of shot!' And my father said: 'Mine too, you clumsy coot!' So they made remarks to each other for a spell; and then Jim said: 'Well, anyway, there's the fox; and I'm full of your shot, and I'm half froze. Let's skin the darned critter and get home.'

"So father agreed; and they went at it. The old dog had come up by then, and was sitting there with an eye on the fox, as a dog will. And father took the front legs and Jim took the hind legs, and they worked fast. And they kept cussing their hurts, and the cold, and each other. But they slit the legs down, and skinned out the tail, and trimmed up the ears and all, knives flying. And when they got about done, Jim, he said:

" 'Look ahere, there's not a bullet in this fox.'

"Well, they looked, and they couldn't find a hole. Only there was a blue streak across the fox's head where a bullet had gone. And that was queer enough, but father said: 'I don't give a hoot. There's bullets enough in me. Skin out his nose and let's go.'

"So they cussed each other some more, and finished it up; and Jim, he heaved the carcass out into the brush, and father slung the skin over his shoulder, and they turned around to start home.

"Well, just about then the old dog let out behind them, and they whirled around. And father always used to say that, mad as they were at each other, they forgot all about it then; and they bust out laughing. He said you couldn't blame them. He said you never saw anything funnier.

"You see, that fox was just stunned. The cold snow must have revived him. Because when my father and Uncle Jim looked around, that skinless fox was going up over the hill like a cat up a tree—and the old dog hot on his heels."

The store rocked with their mirth as Westley stopped. Lee Motley roared, and the Saladines laughed in their silent fashion, and Will Bissell chuckled discreetly behind Proutt's back. Westley himself displayed such surprise at their mirth that they laughed the more; and fat little Jean Bubier shook a finger at Proutt and cried:

"And that will put the bee to your Dan, M'sieu Proutt. That will hold your Dan for one lettle while, I t'ink."

Proutt himself was brick-red with fury; and his eyes were black on Westley; but he pulled himself together, and he laughed . . . shortly.

His eyes did not leave Westley's face. And Lee Motley found a chance to warn the warden a little later. "It was a good joke," he said. "You handed it to him right. But look out for the man, Westley. He's mad."

Westley, still smiling, was nevertheless faintly troubled. "I'm sorry," he said. "I did it for a joke."

"He can't take a joke," said Motley.

The warden nodded, considering. "I'll tell you," he told Motley. "I'll square it with him."

"If it was me," Motley agreed, "I would."

Westley did not like to make enemies. And there had been only the friendliest malice in his jest. He took his measures to soothe Proutt before they left the store that night.

Westley had a dog, a setter, clean-blooded, from one of the country's finest kennels. A New York man who had shot woodcock with the warden the year before had sent the dog as a friendly gift, and Westley accepted it in the same spirit. In its second year and still untrained, it had nevertheless won Westley and won his wife and his children. They all loved the dog, as they loved each other. . . .

Originally this dog had been called Rex. The Westleys changed this name to Reck, which may be short for Reckless, or may be a name by itself. At any rate, it pleased them, and it pleased the dog. . . .

The dog was untrained, and Westley had no time for the arduous work of training. He had meant to send Reck, this fall, to Hepperton, in Liberty; but, to make his amends to

Proutt, he took the latter aside this night and asked Proutt to take the training of the dog.

On longer consideration, he might not have done this; but Westley was a man of impulse and, as has been said, he was anxious to keep Proutt as a friend. Nevertheless, he had no sooner asked Proutt to take the dog than he regretted it, and hoped Proutt would refuse. But the dog trainer only gave a moment to slow consideration, with downcast eyes.

Then he said huskily: "I charge fifty dollars."

"Sure," said Westley.

"He's a well-blooded dog," said Proutt. "I'll come tomorrow and fetch him."

And with no further word—they were outside the store—he drove away. Westley, watching him go, was filled with vague disquiet. He wished he might withdraw; he wished Proutt would change his mind; he wished the trainer might not come next day. . . .

But Proutt did come, and Westley himself bade Reck into the trainer's buggy and watched the dog ride away with wistful eyes turned backward.

Westley's wife was more concerned than he; and he forgot his own anxiety in reassuring her.

There are a thousand methods for the training of a bird dog, and each man prefers his own. There are some dogs which need much training; there are others which require little or none.

Reck was so nobly blooded that the instincts of his craft were deeply bedded in him. On his first day in the alder swamps with Proutt he proved himself to the full. Proutt was a dog beater, as all men know, but he did not beat dogs which obeyed him, and he did not beat Reck. This first day he was merely trying the dog.

Reck found a bird, and took stanch point, steady as a rock.

It was not yet October, the season was not yet open; and so Proutt had no right to shoot. Nevertheless he did walk up this bird, and flushed it from where it lay six feet before Reck's nose, and knocked it over before it topped the alders.

Reck stood at point till the bird rose; when its whistling wings lifted it, his nose followed it upward, followed its fall. . . . But he did not stir, did not break shot; and Proutt, watching, knew that this was indeed a dog.

When the bird had fallen, Proutt said softly: "Reck! Fetch dead bird."

Now, this is in some measure the test of a setter. There are many setters which take a natural point and hold it; there are some few which are also natural retrievers, without training. Reck had been taught by Westley's children to fetch sticks or rocks at command. He knew the word.

He went swiftly forward and brought the woodcock, scarce ruffled, and laid it in Proutt's hand. And Proutt took the bird, and stood still, looking down at Reck with a darkly brooding face. Considering, weighing. . . . After a little he began to curse softly, under his breath; and he turned and stamped out of the alder run, and bade Reck to heel, and went home. And Reck trotted at his heels, tongue out, panting happily. . . .

There are many ways by which the Devil may come at a man. One of them is through hatred, and another way is to put a helpless thing in that man's hands. If the good in him outweighs the bad, well enough; but if the evil has ascendancy, then that man is utterly lost and damned.

Proutt hated Westley; Proutt had in his hands Reck, a dog by Westley well-beloved. And Reck was pliant in Proutt's hands, both because Proutt knew dogs and because Reck was by nature tractable, eager to please, anxious to do that which he was asked to do. The combination presented itself to Proutt full clearly, as he walked his homeward way that day, and it is to be supposed that he fought out what fight there was within himself, during that long walk, and through the evening that followed.

That Proutt had some battle with himself cannot be denied. No man sets out to destroy a soul without first overcoming the scruples which bind him; and there were scruples in Proutt. There must have been. He loved dogs, loved fine dogs, and Reck was fine. Yet the destruction of Reck's honor and reputation and life—these were the ends which Proutt set himself to bring about—at what pain to his own heart no man may fully guess. It can only be known that in the end his hatred overweighed all else—that he threw himself into the thing he meant to do.

Reck, as has been shown, needed no training for his appointed work. Yet Proutt kept him, labored with him daily, for close to four long weeks, as all Fraternity men knew. None saw that training. It was known that Proutt took Reck far over the Sheepscot Ridge, where farms were all deserted; and no man was like to come upon him. But he had done that with dogs before, for woodcock lay thick in Sheepscot Valley. Once or twice men heard the barking of a dog in that valley; and there was a measure of pain in the notes. And three times men met Proutt driving homeward, with Reck lying weary and subdued upon the floor of the buggy, scarce fit to lift his head. It was remarked that Proutt was more dour and morose than ever; and Lee Motley thought the man was aging. . . .

One man only, and that man Jim Saladine, caught some inkling of that which was afoot. Jim was a deer hunter; and toward mid-October, with a shotgun under his arm for luck's sake, but never a buckshot in his cartridge pocket, he went one day into the Sheepscot Valley to search out the land. Deer lay in the swamps there; and Jim sought to locate them against the coming season. He moved slowly and quietly, as his custom was; ears and eyes open. And he saw many things which another man would never have seen.

Two things he saw which had significance. Once, in a muddy patch along the Sheepscot's brim, he came upon a deer's track; and other tracks beside it. A man's track, and a dog's.

Jim studied these tracks. They were sadly muddled; and he could make little of them. But he was sure of this much— that man and dog had been attentive to the tracks of the deer. And this stayed in Jim's mind, because no dog in Fraternity has any business with the track of a deer, and no man may justly set a dog upon such track.

Later that day Jim was to find some explanation for what he had seen. Where Fuller's brook comes into the Sheepscot, there lies an open meadow half a mile long, and half as broad; and near the lower end of the meadow half a dozen alders group about a lone tree in the open. Deer and moose, coming up the Sheepscot Valley, are like to cross the stream below and then traverse this meadow; and Jim Saladine stopped under cover at the meadow's head—it was near dusk—to see what he should see.

He saw what you may see any day along the Sheepscot, and what, by the same token, you may go a weary year without seeing. He saw a deer, a proud buck, come up from the stream and follow the meadow toward where he lay. It passed the isolated alder clump, and something there gave it alarm; for Jim saw its head lift—saw then the quick leap and rush which carried the creature to cover and away. . . .

Saw something else. Out from the alder clump burst a man, driving before him a dog. Dusk was falling, Jim could see their figures only dimly. But this much he saw. The man urged the dog after the deer, with waving arms; and the dog, ever looking backward shamefacedly, trotted slowly off upon the trail, the man still urging from behind.

They slipped into the brush where the deer had gone, and Jim caught no further glimpse of them.

Now, Saladine was an honest man, who loved the deer he hunted; and he was angry. But he was also a just man; and he could not be sure whom he had seen. So it was that he kept a still tongue, and waited, and through the weeks that followed he watched, patiently enough, for what should come.

He meant, in that hour, to take a hand.

With a week of October left, Proutt took Reck home to Westley. Westley was not there, but Mrs. Westley marked Proutt's lowering eye, and was frightened of the man, and told Westley so when he came. But Westley was well enough pleased to have Reck back again; and he bade her forget Proutt.

Proutt had been, thus far, somewhat favored by fortune. The business of his office had taken Westley away from Fraternity for two weeks at a time, so that Proutt had had full time to do with Reck as he chose. Fraternity knew nothing of what had happened, though Jim Saladine may have guessed. There was one night at Will's store when Jim and Proutt were near fisticuffs. Proutt had brought Dan with him to the store; and Jim, studying the surly dog, asked:

"Dan ever notice a deer, Proutt?"

Proutt exclaimed profanely. "No," he said.

"I was over in the Sheepscot, t'other day," said Jim evenly. "See tracks where a dog had been after a deer."

"More like it was one of these setters," Proutt declared, watching them all from beneath lowered lids. "They'll kill a deer, or a sheep, give 'em a chance."

"It was hound's tracks," Jim persisted mildly; and something in Jim's tone, or in Proutt's own heart, made the trainer boil into fury, so that he strode toward Saladine. But Will Bissell came between, and the matter passed.

Proutt, before this, had taken Reck home; and the Westleys made much of the dog. Reck had affable and endearing little tricks of his own. He had a way of giving welcome, drawing back his upper lip so that his teeth showed as though in a snarl, yet panting with dog laughter all the time; and he had a way of talking, with high whines of delight, or throaty growls that ran the scale. And he would lie beside Westley, or beside Westley's wife, and paw at them until they held his paw in their hands, when he would go contentedly enough to sleep.

They thought the dog was unhappy when he came home to them. He had a slinking, shamed way about him. At first Westley supposed Proutt had whipped him; but Reck showed no fear of a whip in Westley's hands. After two or three days this furtiveness passed away and Reck was the joyously affectionate creature he had always been. So the Westleys forgot his first attitude of guilt, and loved him ardently as men and women will love a dog.

Westley had opportunity for one day's hunting with him, and Reck never faltered at the task to which he had been born and bred.

He had one fault. Chained, he would bark at the least alarm, in a manner to wake the neighborhood. So Westley had never kept him chained. It was not the way of Fraternity to keep dogs in the house of nights; so Reck slept in the woodshed, and Westley knocked a plank loose and propped it, leaving Reck an easy avenue to go out or in. It was this custom of Westley's which gave Proutt the chance for which he had laid his plans.

October had gone; November had come. This was in the days when woodcock might be shot in November if you could find them. But most men who went into the woods bore rifles; for it was open season for deer. Now and then you might hear the snapping crash of a thirty-thirty in Whitcher Swamp, or at one of the crossings, or—if you went so far—in the alder vales along the Sheepscot. And one day in the middle of the month, when the ground was frozen hard, Proutt came to Nick Westley's home.

He came at noon, driving his old buggy. Westley was at

dinner when he heard Proutt drive into the yard; and he went to the door and bade the dog trainer come in. But Proutt shook his head, and his eyes were somber.

"You come out, Westley," he said. "I've a word for you."

There was something in Proutt's tone which disturbed Westley. He put on his mackinaw, and drew his cap down about his ears, and went out into the yard. Reck had been asleep on the doorstep when Proutt appeared; he had barked a single bark. But now he was gone into the shed, out of sight; and when Westley came near Proutt's buggy, the dog trainer asked:

"Did you see Reck sneak away?"

Westley was angry; and he was also shaken by a sudden tremor of alarm. He said hotly enough: "Reck never sneaks. He did not sneak away."

"He knows I saw him," said Proutt. "He heard me yell."

Westley asked with narrowing eyes: "What are you talking about? Where did you see him?"

"This morning," Proutt declared. "Scant daylight. Down in the Swamp."

Westley stood very still, trying to remember whether he had seen Reck early that morning. And he could only remember, with a shocking certainty, that Reck had not been at home when he came out of the house to do his chores. He had called and got no answer; and it may have been half an hour before the dog appeared. It had disturbed Westley at the time; and he scolded Reck for self-hunting. But any dog will range the home farm in the morning hours, and Westley had not taken the matter seriously.

Proutt's words, and his tone more than his words, made the matter very serious indeed. Westley forced himself to ask: "What were you doing in the Swamp?"

"I was after a deer," said Proutt; and when Westley remained silent, Proutt added huskily: "So was Reck."

Westley cried: "That's a lie." But his own voice sounded

strange and unnatural in his ears. He would not believe. Yet he knew that other dogs had chased deer in the past, and would again. He had himself shot half a dozen. It was the law; and he was the instrument of the law. And this was the very bitterness of Proutt's accusation; for if it were true, then he must shoot Reck. And Westley would as soon have shot one of his own blood as the dog he loved.

In the little instant of silence that followed upon his word, he saw all this, too clearly. And in spite of his love for Reck, and in spite of his ardent longing to believe that Proutt had lied, he feared desperately that the man spoke truth. Westley's wife would never have believed; for a woman refuses to believe any evil of those she loves. She is loyal by refusing to believe; a man may believe and be loyal still.

Westley did not know whether to believe or not; but he knew that he was terribly afraid. He told Proutt: "That's a lie!" And Proutt, after a long moment, clucked to his horse and started on. Westley called after him: "Wait!"

Proutt stopped his horse; and Westley asked; "What are you going to do?"

"You're game warden," Proutt told him sullenly. "Nobody around here can make you act, less'n you're a mind to. But I've told you what's going on."

Westley was sweating in the cold, and said pitifully: "Proutt, are you sure?"

"Yes," said Proutt; and Westley cried: "What did you see?"

"I had a deer marked," said Proutt slowly. "He'd been feeding under an old apple tree down there. I was there before day this morning, figuring to get a shot at him. Crep' in quiet. Come day, I couldn't see him. But after a spell I heard a smashing in the brush, and he come out through an open, and was away before I could shoot. And hot after him came Reck."

"How far away?" Westley asked.

"No more'n ten rod."

"You couldn't be sure."

"Damn it, man, I know Reck. Besides, I wouldn't want to say it was him, would I? He's a grand dog."

"What did you do?" Westley asked.

"Yelled at him to come in."

"Did he stop?"

"Stopped for one look, and then one jump into the brush and away he went."

Westley was almost convinced; he turned to call Reck, with some curious and half-formed notion that he might catechize the dog himself. But when he turned, he found Reck at his side; and the setter was standing steadily, legs stiff and proud like a dog on show, eyes fixed on Proutt. There was no guilt in his attitude; nor was there accusation. There was only steady pride and self-respect; and Westley, at sight of him, could not believe this damning thing.

He said slowly: "Look at him, Proutt. If this were true, he'd be ashamed, and crawling. You saw some other dog."

Proutt shook his head. "He's a wise, bold dog, is Reck. Wise as you and me. He'll face it out if he can."

Westley pulled himself together, dropping one hand on Reck's head. "I don't believe it, Proutt," he said. "But I'm going to make sure."

"I am sure," said Proutt. "You can do as you please. But don't ask me to keep my mouth shut. You was quick enough to shoot Jackson's dog when you caught her on that doe."

"I know," said Westley; and his face was white. "I'll be as quick with Reck, when I'm sure."

"You'll take pains not to get sure."

Westley held his voice steady. "Did you ever have to call Reck off of deer tracks?"

"No."

"Then he's never been taught not to run them?"

"Neither had Jackson's dog."

"What I mean," said Westley, "is this. He doesn't know it's wrong to run deer."

"That's no excuse."

"I'm not excusing him."

Proutt swore. "Well, what are you doing?"

"I'm going to take him into the swamp and find a deer," said Westley slowly. "See what he does. He's never been taught not to run them. So he'll run any that we find. If it's in him to do it, he'll take after them—"

Proutt nodded; and there was a certain triumph in his eyes. "You take your gun along," he said. "You're going to need that gun."

Westley, white and steady, said: "I'll take the gun. Will you come along?"

"Sure."

"Do you know where we can find a deer?"

"No; not this time o' day."

Westley turned toward the house. "Wait," he said. "I'll get my gun; and we'll go pick up Jim Saladine. He'll know."

Proutt nodded. "I'll wait," he agreed.

Westley went into the house. Reck stood on the doorstep. Proutt, waiting, watched Reck with a flickering, deadly light in his sullen eyes.

Saladine listened silently to Westley's request; but he looked at Proutt with an eye before which Proutt uneasily turned away his head. Nevertheless, being by nature a taciturn man, he made no comment or suggestion. He only said: "I can find a deer."

"Where?" Westley asked.

"Over in the Sheepscot," said Saladine. "I've got mine for this season; but I know some hardwood ridges over there where they're like to be feeding, come evening."

Proutt said uneasily: "Hell, there's a deer nearer than Sheepscot."

"Where?" asked Saladine.

"Everywhere."

"We ain't got time to cover that much territory today," the hunter said mildly. "If the Sheepscot suits, I'll go along. I'm most sure we'll pick up deer."

Westley asked: "Do you think I'm testing Reck fair?"

Saladine spat. "Yes, I'd say so," he agreed.

"I've got work to do," Proutt still objected. "Sheepscot's a danged long way."

"I want you to come," said Westley.

So Proutt assented at last; and they set off in his team. He and Westley in the front seat, Saladine and Reck behind. A five-mile drive over the Sheepscot Ridge. "Past Mac's Corner," Saladine told them; and they went that way.

The road took them by Proutt's house; and old Dan, Proutt's hound, came out to bark at them, and saw Proutt, and tried to get into the buggy. Proutt bade him back to the house; then, as an afterthought, got out and shut the hound indoors. "Don't want him following," he said.

Saladine's eyes were narrow with thought, but he made no comment, and they moved on their way.

That part of Maine in which Fraternity lies is a curious study for geologists. A good many centuries ago, when the great glaciers graved this land, they slid down from north to south into the sea, and in their sliding plowed deep furrows, so that the country is cut up by ridges, running almost true north and south, and ending in peninsulas with bays between. Thus the coast line is jagged as a saw.

These ridges run far up into the State; and the Sheepscot Ridge is as bold as any one of them. There is no break in it; and it herds the little waterways down into Sheepscot River, and guides the river itself south till it meets the sea. There are trout in Sheepscot; and thirty years ago the valley was full of farms and mills; but these farms are for the most part deserted now, and the mills are gone, leaving only shattered dams to mark the spots where they stood. The valley is a tangle of second-growth timber, broken here and there by ancient meadows through which brooks meander. Here dwells every wild thing that the region knows.

Proutt's old buggy climbed the long road up the eastern slope of the ridge; and the somber beauty of the countryside lay outspread behind them. The sun was falling lower; the shadows were lengthening; and a cold wind blew across the land. Across George's Valley and George's Lake lay the lower hills, the Appleton Ridge beyond, and far southeast the higher domes of Megunticook and the Camden Hills. The bay itself could not be seen, but the dark top of Blue Hill showed, twenty miles beyond the bay; and Mount Desert, ten miles farther still. . . .

The men had no eyes for these beauties. They rode in silence, watching the road ahead. And they passed through Liberty, and past Mac's Corner, and so up to top the ridge at last. Paused there to breathe Proutt's horse.

Back at Proutt's home, about the time they were in Liberty, some one had opened the door of the shed in which old Dan was locked; and the hound, watching his chance, scuttled out into the open. What well-founded habit prompted him can only be guessed; certain it is that he wheeled, never heeding the calls from behind him, and took the road by which Proutt had gone, hard on his master's trail.

If the dog trainer had known this, matters might have turned out differently. But Proutt could not know.

The road from Sheepscot Ridge down into Sheepscot Valley is for the most part rough and little used. An occasional farmer comes this way; an occasional fisherman drops from the steep descent to the bridge. But the frost has thrown boulders up across the road; and grass grows between the ruts, and the young hardwood crowds close on either side. Down this road, at Saladine's direction, Proutt turned; and the westering sun shone through the leafless branches and laid a bright mosaic before the feet of the horse.

Halfway down the hill Saladine spoke. "Let's light out," he said. "We'll find something up along this slope."

Westley nodded; and Proutt, after a moment's hesitation, stopped his horse. They got out, and Reck danced about their feet. Proutt tied the horse to a sapling beside the road; and they climbed the ruined stone wall and turned into the wood. Westley alone had a gun; the others were unarmed.

The course Saladine set for them was straight along the slope, moving neither up nor down; and the three men, accustomed to the woods, went quickly. Westley spoke to Reck now and then. His only word was the hunter's command. "Get in there," he said. "Get in. Go on." And Reck ranged forward, and up, and down, covering a front of half a dozen rods as they advanced. Westley was in the middle. Saladine was below, Proutt above the other two.

Westley had suggested putting his hunting bell on Reck; but Proutt negatived that with a caustic word. "He'd know, then, you wanted birds," he said. "And, anyways, it'd scare the deer." So they followed the dog by sight or by the stirring of his feet among the leaves; and at times he was well ahead of them, and at times when he moved more slowly they were close upon his heels. At such moments Westley held them back till Reck should work ahead.

Whether Reck had any knowledge of what was in their minds, no man can say. There were moments when they saw he was uncertain, when he turned to look inquiringly back at them. But for the most part he worked steadily back and forth as a good dog will, quartering the ground by inches. And always he progressed along the ridge, and always they followed him. And Saladine, down the slope, watched Proutt as they moved on.

No man spoke, save that Westley urged Reck softly on when the dog turned back to look at them. And at the last,

After a rod or two, Reck stopped.

when they saw that Reck had found game, it needed no word to bring the three together, two or three rods behind the dog.

Reck, as the gunners say, was "marking game." Nose down, he moved forward, foot by foot; and now and then he stopped for long seconds motionless, as though at point; but always he moved forward again. And Westley felt the cold sweat upon his forehead; and he looked at Proutt and saw the dog trainer licking his tight lips. Only Saladine kept a steady eye upon the dog and searched the thickets ahead.

After a rod or two Reck stopped, and this time he did not move. And Westley whispered to the others: "Walk it up, whatever it is. Move in." So the men went slowly forward, eyes aching with the strain of staring into the shadows of the wood.

When Reck took his point he was well ahead of them. He held it while they came up beside him; and then, as they passed where the dog stood, something plunged in the brush ahead, and they all saw the swift flash of brown and the bobbing white tail as a buck deer drove straight away from them along the slope. And Proutt cried triumphantly:

"A deer, by God! I said it. I told you so. Shoot, Westley. Damn you, shoot!"

Westley stood still as still, and his heart was sunk a hundred fathoms deep. His hand was shaking and his eyes were blurred with tears. For Reck, who had no rightful concern with anything that roved the woods save the creatures which go on the wing, had marked a deer. Enough to damn him! Had hunted deer! . . .

He tried to lift the gun, but Saladine spoke sharply. "Hold on. Look at the dog. He didn't chase the deer."

Westley realized then that Reck was, in fact, still marking game, moving slowly on ahead of them. But Proutt cried: "He'd smelled it; he didn't see it go. Or there's another ahead."

"He didn't chase the deer," said Saladine. Westley, without speaking, moved forward behind the dog. And of a sudden his heart could beat again.

For they came to where the buck had been lying, to his bed, still warm. And Reck passed over this warm bed, where the deer scent was so strong the men could almost catch it themselves; passed over this scent as though it did not exist, and swung, beyond, to the right, and up the slope. The buck had gone forward and down.

"He's not after deer," said Saladine.

They knew what he was after in the next instant; for wings drummed ahead of them, and four partridges got up, huge, fleeting shadows in the darkening woods. And Reck's nose followed them in flight till they were gone, then swung back to Westley, wrinkling curiously, as though he asked:

"Why did you not shoot?"

Westley went down on his knees and put his arms about the dog's neck; and then he came to his feet uncertainly as Proutt exclaimed: "Hell, he was after deer. He knew we were watching. Took the birds."

Westley tried to find a word, but Saladine, that silent man, stepped forward.

"Westley," he said, "wait a minute. You, Proutt, be still."

They looked at him uncertainly, Proutt growling. And Saladine spat on the ground as though he tasted the unclean. "I've kept my mouth shut. Wanted to see. Meant to tell it in the end. Westley, Proutt broke your dog."

Westley nodded. "Yes." He looked at Proutt.

"He broke him to run deer."

Westley began to tremble, and he could not take his eyes from Saladine; and Proutt broke out in a roaring oath, till Saladine turned slowly upon him.

The deer hunter went on: "I waited to see. I knowed what would come; but I wanted to see. A bird dog's bred to birds. If he's bred right, it's in him. Reck's bred right. You can make him run deer. Proutt did. But you can't make him like it. Birds is his meat. You saw that just now. He didn't pay any heed to that buck; but he did pay heed to the pa'tridge."

Proutt cried: "Damn you, Saladine, you can't say a thing like that."

Saladine cut in: "I saw you. Month ago. Down by Fuller's Brook. A deer crossed there, up into the meadow. You was in the alders with Reck, and you tried to set him on. He wouldn't run, and you drove him. I saw you, Proutt."

Westley looked down at Reck; and he looked at Proutt, the trainer; and he looked back at Reck again. There was something in Reck's eyes which made him hot and angry; there was a pleading something in Reck's slowly wagging tail. . . . And Westley turned to Proutt, cool enough now; and he said:

"I can see it now, Proutt. I've known there was something, felt there was something." He laughed joyously. "Why, Proutt, you man who knows dogs. Didn't you know you could not kill the soul and the honor of a dog like mine? Reck is a thoroughbred. He knows his work. And you—"

He moved a little toward the other. "Proutt," he said, "I'm going to lick you till you can't stand."

Proutt's big head lowered between his shoulders. "So—" he said.

And Westley stepped toward him.

Saladine said nothing; Reck did not stir; and the woods about them were as still as still. It was in this silence, before a blow could be struck, that they heard the pound of running feet in the timber above them; and Saladine said swiftly: "Deer!"

He moved, with the word, half a dozen paces back by the way they had come, to an old wood road they had crossed, and stood there, looking up the slope. Westley and Proutt forgot each other and followed him; and Reck stayed close at Westley's heel. They could hear the beating feet more plainly now; and Saladine muttered:

"Scared. Something chasing it."

On the word, abruptly startling them, the deer came into view—a doe, running swiftly and unwearied. Striking the wood road, the creature followed the easier going, down the slope toward them; and because they were so still it failed to discover the men till it was scarce two rods away. Sighting them then, the doe stopped an instant, then lightly leaped into the brush at one side, and was gone.

The men did not look after the deer; they waited to see what pursued it. And after a moment Saladine's face grimly hardened, and Westley's became somber and grave, and Proutt turned pale as ashes.

For, lumbering down the hill upon the deer's hot trail, came Dan, that hound which Proutt had shut away at home —came Dan, hot on the trail as Proutt had taught him.

The dog saw them, as the deer had done, and would have swung aside. But Proutt cried, in a broken voice: "Dan, come in."

So came the hound to heel, sullenly and slowly, eyes off into the wood where the doe had gone; and for a moment no one spoke, till Saladine slowly drawled:

"Westley, give Proutt your gun."

Westley did not speak. He was immensely sorry for Proutt, and all his anger at the man had gone. Proutt looked old, and shaken, and weary; and he had dropped his heavy hand across Dan's neck. He caught Westley's eye and said harshly: "To hell with your gun. I'll use my own."

An instant more they stood; then Westley turned to Saladine. "Jim, let's go," he said. And Saladine nodded, and they moved away. Reck at Westley's heels. After a moment, an odd panic in his voice, Proutt called after them: "Wait, I'll ride you home."

But Saladine answered: "I'll walk!" And Westley did not speak at all. He and Reck and the deer hunter went steadily upon their way.

The sun was setting; and dark shadows filtered through the trees to hide old Proutt where he still stood beside his dog.

WORLD *Junior* LIBRARY

Exciting, action-filled, inspiring and always engross-
ing, WORLD JUNIOR LIBRARY books will delight
all boys and girls who love good reading. These are
quality books by famous authors, in handsome, cloth-
bound library editions.

TITLES NOW AVAILABLE

JILL'S VICTORY *by Elisa Bialk*

THE SUN-DOG TRAIL *by Jack London*

SMOKE BELLEW *by Jack London*

JEAN CRAIG GRADUATE NURSE
by Kay Lyttleton

PAT'S HARMONY *by Page Cooper*

GHOST GABLES *by Mildred A. Wirt*

THE PAINTED SHIELD *by Mildred A. Wirt*

WILD STALLION *by Bud Murphy*

BULLARD OF THE SPACE PATROL
by Malcolm Jameson

FAVORITE DOG STORIES
edited by Marguerite Bloch

COMANCHE *by David Appel*

MONKEY SHINES *by Earl S. Miers*

THE WORLD PUBLISHING COMPANY

CLEVELAND AND NEW YORK